Uncorked

ANDREW GREY

Dreamspinner Press

Published by
Dreamspinner Press
4760 Preston Road
Suite 244-149
Frisco, TX 75034
http://www.dreamspinnerpress.com/

Uncorked

Cover Design by Mara McKennen

ISBN: 978-1-61581-297-4

Printed in the United States of America
First Edition
November, 2009

eBook edition available
eBook ISBN: 978-1-61581-298-1

For everyone at Central Pennsylvania Romance Writers,
thank you for all your support and fun. You are truly an inspiration.

And to Dominic, without whose support I couldn't write at all.

CHAPTER 1

"COME on in," the professor said. Bobby Bielecki walked into the familiar office and closed the door behind him. Gregory Hansen sat behind his desk, framed by mounds of papers and books, the shelves above him filled with pots, clay models, bronzes, and even glass, a collection from his thirty years as a professor of fine art. "What can I help you with today?" he asked.

"I need to make sure I have everything set so I can graduate after next term," Bobby said, opening his messenger bag and locating the paper he needed. "Here's my expected schedule."

The handsome, older man took the paper and studied it carefully before pulling out a drawer and fishing in his files. "Let's run through the requirements." Pulling out the degree checklist, he began clicking keys on his computer and adding grades beside the classes. "This is easy. If I ever forgot how to write an A, you'd be in trouble."

Bobby smiled as the man continued working. He wasn't a straight-A student, mainly because of the general education requirements, but he was a very good student. He smiled to himself as he thought of all those evenings spent with Kenny around the kitchen table, Sean helping them with their homework when they couldn't help each other.

Professor Hansen finished with the computer and began filling in classes from Bobby's expected schedule for next semester. "It looks like you've got all the classes covered. Have you thought about your senior project?" he asked, handing Bobby the completed check sheet for his reference.

"I've tried, but nothing really comes to mind."

The professor sat back in his chair. "You've got a few months before it's due, but you should start thinking about it."

"I know. I just haven't been very inspired lately. Is there such a thing as artist's block?" Bobby tried to smile, but he'd been feeling this way for a while, and he hated it. Everything was a struggle. "I've tried wandering the city, experiencing different things." The professor looked down his nose, a very concerned look on his face. "I haven't tried anything stupid," Bobby said as he rolled his eyes, but after some of the things he'd seen the last few years, he understood the professor's reaction.

"Inspiration can sometimes be fickle and fleeting, and at other times, a bounty of riches so fruitful you can't work fast enough to capture it all."

"I know. There was a time when I could pick up my sketchbook, and my hands would draw on their own. I didn't need to think. It would just happen. Now, I sit for hours sometimes and nothing comes."

"Let me ask you a question," the professor said, leaning forward. "When was the last time you felt like that? When things came to you easily and freely."

"It's hard to remember." Bobby sighed. "It's been a while." *Quite a while, if I were being honest.*

"That seems to fit with what I've been hearing from your professors. They all say you're very talented, bordering on greatness, but there's something lacking." Hansen leaned forward again. "As artists, we have to put ourselves into our art; give it everything we have. I think you may be holding back some part of you. What are you afraid of? What is it you're holding back?"

"I wish I knew. There are times when I can really feel something, but then it fades. I know this has to come from me, and what you're telling me isn't a surprise. I just can't figure it out."

Professor Hansen smiled a broad smile that lit his entire face. "I think you're looking in the wrong place, using the wrong method." Bobby sat forward, listening intently. "The answer isn't in your mind—it's in your emotions. You're trying to figure your way down a path where you need to feel your way. Let your emotions guide you. Find out what makes you feel strongly and then follow it."

"Thank you." Bobby got up to leave. He could see another student outside the frosted glass door.

"I'll tell you one thing," Professor Hansen said. "When you do find what unlocks the emotional well inside, hold onto it for dear life and don't let go, no matter what."

"I won't, professor. Thank you." Bobby opened the door and walked into the hallway and down to the elevators, passing a number of students who either said hello or waved. It seemed a number of students were doing the same thing he was. Taking the elevator to the first floor, he walked across the polished tile floor toward the exit, slipping on his coat before stepping outside. The cold wind right off Lake Michigan easily cut through to his skin, and he hurried along the sidewalk to the residence hall.

He was chilled to the bone in the ten minutes he was outside—thank God it wasn't snowing yet. He made a quick stop to get his mail and then called for the elevator, riding it to the top floor.

When he opened the door to his room, he heard, "How'd it go?" Raphael—his real name, poor boy—sat at Bobby's drafting table, working on an assignment for class. Their room was the epitome of what an art student's dorm room should look like: a drafting table in one corner, an easel in another. At one time, there had even been a potter's wheel in there, and before that, an antique printing press Tyler had found for Bobby to use on a project.

"Just as I expected. I have all the classes I need, and my advisor urged me to start thinking about my senior project." Bobby flopped down on the small sofa, picking up his sketchpad and doodling a drawing of Raphael before dropping the pad on the table.

"Still feeling blocked?" Raphael asked.

"I guess. He suggested I'm looking in the wrong place."

Raphael put down his pencils and stepped from behind the table, sitting next to him on the sofa. "Maybe he's right and maybe you're just feeling unsettled and nervous for some reason. I know a good cure for that." Raphael smirked as he ran his hand up Bobby's leg and then quickly dashed across the room as a pillow came flying at his head.

"Tease!" Bobby shouted. He began laughing as his roommate picked up the pillow and heaved it back at him.

"Slut!" The pillow flew back across the room, hitting Raphael's hip.

"Ballgazer!" Bobby called, as Raphael's throw caught him square in the chest.

"Cum-dumpster!" Bobby was laughing too hard to throw the pillow back, and Raphael lifted his arms in triumph. "I won. It took three years, but I won!" Bobby thought he was going to do a Snoopy dance right there in the middle of the room.

He and Raphael had met when Sean and Sam first dropped Bobby off. When they'd walked into the room, Raphael's eyes had bugged as Bobby introduced himself and his two dads. As soon as Sam and Sean left, the questioning began. "Are you gay? Was it way cool to have two dads?" Bobby had answered the questions, firing back some of his own, and they were immediately friends.

They'd shared a room for more than three years and a bed for about six months during sophomore year. Most people would think the affair, or "affair-ette," as Raphael referred to it, would have ended their friendship, but it didn't. They both realized at about the same time that it wouldn't work. Bobby went back to sleeping in his own bed, and that was that. It did have one side effect that neither of them talked about: they never brought other guys back to their room. It was just one of those unwritten, unspoken rules they both understood.

Not that there'd been a parade of men for either of them. They'd both had brief flings, but no one captured their attention. That is, until lately. Raphael had been seeing a man a few years older than he was, and they really seemed to be hitting it off. Bobby wasn't sure if he liked this guy, but Raph seemed to be happy, so he didn't say anything.

"Did Simon invite you to spend the term break with him?" Bobby asked.

Raphael beamed. "He did. But my folks would have a fit, so I'm spending a few days with them and the rest of the time with Simon. He said he'd take me to New York for a few days."

"Sounds like fun." He tried to keep his expression happy, but he couldn't help being suspicious. Simon always made these grandiose plans that either got canceled or changed to something else.

The phone interrupted their conversation. Raph answered it and then handed it to Bobby. "It's your dad."

"Hey, Dad, what's up?"

"Are you coming home during the term break?" Sean sounded so excited.

"Absolutely. I'm looking forward to spending some time with you and Sam. Why?" His inquiry was met by silence, which meant that something was definitely up, and Sean was feeling guilty for some reason.

"Well, Sam got one of those weeks off, and I was hoping you'd agree to work in the store for me."

Shit, Bobby hated it when Sean sounded guilty for asking something simple. He had always put Bobby and Kenny first. "Of course. Are you guys going away?" Bobby replied hopefully. He couldn't remember them ever going on a real vacation together.

"Sam's been looking into booking a week in the Caribbean, and I was hoping…."

Bobby felt his smile deep down. "Tell Sam to book it. I'll work in the store while you're gone. No sweat." Then a thought occurred to him. "When's Kenny's break?"

"I think it's the same week. I'll call and see if he can help too." Sean sounded so happy.

Manning the store for a week was the least Bobby could do. Part of him really wanted to see Kenny—the secret part that still hoped—and part of him was nervous about the reception he'd get. Over the last few years, their relationship had grown cooler and more distant. They saw each other only occasionally, and Bobby knew that it was as much his fault as Kenny's. Even during the summer, Bobby had internships and Kenny often stayed in school or went to summer programs with police departments. Bobby focused his attention back on Sean and they talked a little longer before hanging up.

"Going home?" Raphael asked, sitting back behind the drafting table, hard at work again.

"Yup." This time Bobby had a huge smile on his face. Maybe going home would give him the inspiration he needed. There was a part of him that still hoped he'd win the struggle for Kenny's heart.

KENNY hung up the phone, a smile on his face. "What's got you so happy?" his roommate asked, barely looking up from cleaning his gun. It was one of his favorite pastimes—he did it daily. When Kenny had first met Zach a few years earlier, his first thought was that the guy was the human incarnation of Tackleberry from the *Police Academy* movies that Sean loved. Once he got to know Zach, Kenny realized that his first impression was right on. The man was a gun fanatic. Even though he'd never seen it, Kenny swore the man slept with a gun under his pillow.

"That was my dad. He asked if I was going home for break. It seems they want me to help in the wine store while they're on vacation."

"Bummer." Zach dragged the word out into a sigh. "Weren't you and Clay planning to go to one of those water hotels in the Dells that week?"

Shit! In his happiness for Sean and Sam, Kenny had completely forgotten. "I'll have to call and cancel. Sean and Sam are going on their first vacation alone that I can remember, and I'm going to help them."

"Will your faggy brother be there?" He never looked up from his gun cleaning. Kenny thanked God that Zach had agreed that all ammunition be kept in a locked box. After all, the man cleaned his gun right there in their room. At least Kenny knew it wasn't loaded.

"I'm gay too, Zach, and I don't appreciate that type of language." He turned to stare at his roommate, who actually looked up from his cleaning.

"But you're cool—he's so femmy." He said it without malice, like he was just stating a fact.

Kenny walked over to the sofa and pulled the gun out of Zach's hand, setting it on the table. "I'll say this once and only once." He leaned forward putting his face in Zach's. "Bobby was abandoned by his mother, spent months in foster homes, and lived on the streets, all before he was fifteen. That femmy man has been through hell and saw me through the hell of my father's death." He moved his face close enough to smell Zach's bad breath. "He's seen things that would curl your butch machismo hair."

Zach raised his hand in surrender. "Okay, dude, I give. You hardly ever talk about him, so I thought you didn't really like him. Is *Bobby* going to be there?"

Kenny stepped back and picked up the gun from the table, handing it back to Zach. "Yes, he is." The reason he didn't talk about Bobby wasn't because he didn't like him, but because talking about him made him remember the fun they used to have and how strained their relationship was now. Kenny actually found himself looking forward to seeing him again, especially since he was going to get to spend an entire week alone with him. When he'd first left for college, he'd missed Bobby terribly. It took him about three months before he realized that Bobby was his first love, but by then they were hundreds of miles and two universities apart.

That first Christmas he'd been a fool and kicked Bobby away when he'd tried to sleep with him. Kenny was sure he'd done the right thing, but he knew he'd been way too abrupt and harsh. Bobby had done what he'd asked, but the next morning, he couldn't look him in the eye, and right after New Year's, Bobby left and went back to school early.

Kenny had regretted that ever since, and Bobby hadn't attempted to get close again. Kenny knew he'd hurt their friendship, and he'd hurt the one person he loved and who loved him. Since then, they'd seen each other, but they'd kept their mental and emotional distance.

A knock interrupted his thoughts and he opened the door. Kenny's current boyfriend Clay breezed into the room. "I just made the reservations for the Dells." He leaned in and kissed Kenny softly before resuming his speech. "It's going to be so great." His deep voice resonated through the room.

Kenny tried to interject, "Clay," but Clay barely paused to breathe. "The place I found has huge water slides, and I got us a whirlpool tub."

"Clay." Kenny said it a little louder and more forcefully. He must have heard him this time because he finally paused in his recitation. "Sean called, and he needs me at home that week. He and Sam are going on vacation, and they asked if I could help watch the store while they were gone."

"Can't Bobby do it?" Clay looked so disappointed that Kenny paused for a second, trying to figure out if there was a way he could do both. He was a sucker for those eyes and that hurt look.

"He'll be there too."

As soon as the words were out of Kenny's mouth, he could see a change come over Clay. His eyes hardened, and the lips that looked so cute a second ago nearly disappeared. "So that's the way it is?"

Kenny squinted. "What are you talking about?"

Clay looked mad enough to spit nails. "What am I talking about? Jesus, you really don't know do you?" He shook his head. "You're really sick, you know that?" Clay turned to Zach, "You better be careful, sleeping in the same room with him every night." To his credit Zach just waved Clay off, but Kenny was riveted, wondering what Clay was driving at. "At night when we're sleeping together—"

Zach put his hands over his ears and began to recite, "Too much information, too much information."

Clay looked at Kenny, ignoring Zach completely, "In the middle of the night, you moan and whimper Bobby's name like he's your lover."

Kenny was appalled. He had absolutely no idea his inner thoughts were escaping while he slept. He never remembered his dreams, but he must have been dreaming about Bobby. "I had no idea."

Clay turned and walked to the door. "Don't worry about the reservations. I'm sure I can find someone to go with me—someone who'll call out for *me* in his sleep." With those parting words, he stepped out into the hall, slamming the door behind him.

"Is he gone?" Zach asked. "Can I put my hands down?" Kenny nodded and Zach went back to his gun. "Did you just break up?" Kenny nodded again. "That's too bad." Zach put the gun away. "Wanna go to State Street for dinner? You could probably use a drink, and I could use a chance to meet some ladies." He actually bobbed his head slightly, like he was being really cool.

Kenny felt terrible and hurt. He'd really liked Clay, and even though they'd only been going out for about six weeks, he was going to miss him. Clay was fun and a little wild, something Kenny was not. His goal was to follow in his dad's footsteps and become a police officer in the Milwaukee Police Department, and he knew he had to have a spotless record to be considered. That meant staying away from many of the temptations of college life, not that he minded too much.

"Yeah, let's go. I could use an evening out, and I'd like to look for something for Sam and Sean."

"Okay." They grabbed their coats and left the tiny apartment, walking toward downtown. "Who knows, maybe you'll get lucky tonight and meet the woman who'll turn you straight." Zach started laughing as he pulled the door closed behind them.

Kenny chuckled. "And maybe you'll get lucky and meet the man who'll turn you gay." Kenny began laughing harder as Zach started to cough hard, doubling over in shock. He just couldn't help himself. The expression on Zach's face was enough for Kenny to know that Zach would never, ever try that joke again. "Come on, let's go." Patting Zach on the back, "Breathe, ya big redneck, breathe." Zach finally stopped coughing and they continued down the stairs.

CHAPTER 2

THE last exam for the semester was done, and he'd turned in his final class projects. As Bobby walked across the small campus to the residence hall, he almost began whistling. Just one semester to go, and he was done, at least with his bachelor's degree. A number of his professors were urging him to stay on for his master's. His painting professor had even told him he'd hire him as his teaching and lab assistant if he'd consider it. Bobby wasn't sure what he wanted to do beyond finishing his final semester and completing his senior project.

Opening the door to his room, he wasn't surprised to see Raphael already there, zipping up his suitcase. "My dad's already waiting for me," he said, wrapping Bobby in a vise-grip hug. "Enjoy the break, and I'll see you in a few weeks."

"Have a good time in New York." To Bobby's surprise, Simon had actually come through. He'd even gone so far as to give Raphael a plane ticket. "And take lots of pictures."

"I will, don't worry." Raphael hoisted his suitcase and lugged it out of the room, the door closing with a bang behind him. Bobby swung into action, pulling his case out of the closet and beginning to fill it. He also packed his laptop bag and sketchbooks. Taking one last look through the room, he grabbed his things and left, heading toward the elevator. Leaving the building, he dragged his suitcase to the curb and hailed a cab to take him to the train station.

The train to Milwaukee took a little over an hour, and soon he was outside again, standing in front of the station, trying to decide what he wanted to do. There were taxis at the curb, but he didn't have a great deal of money, and while he knew Sean would give him whatever he needed, he didn't want to ask. The weather was cold but sunny, so he decided to walk. He could use the exercise anyway. Adjusting his load, he began walking across the street.

The store was bustling when Bobby walked through the front door. Customers were selecting their purchases, and Katie and his dad were helping them. It looked the same, but different.

"Bobby!"

He barely had time to drop his luggage before he was pulled into a big hug, which he returned happily. "Hi, Katie, how are you?" God, it felt good to be home—and the store felt like home, always had.

"I'm good." She released him and stepped back, her entire face glowing.

"So how much longer?"

She rubbed her distended belly. "Three more months. I can't wait."

"Have you picked out names?" She must have had this conversation a million times.

"Not yet, but we know it's a boy. The sonogram was definite. Stan didn't want to know, but I did, and since I'm carrying it, I won." She smirked as she returned to the counter to ring up a customer. "He's thrilled about it, by the way." Bobby could tell she was thrilled about it as well.

Bobby saw his dad emerge from the back room, a load of wine cases on a trolley. "You're just in time to stock shelves." Sean's eyes gleamed as he teased.

"Let me put my stuff in the office, and I'll help." Bobby knew Sean wasn't serious, but he was ready to help anyway. He'd been filling shelves and preparing stock for display for more than five years. Picking up his suitcase and other bags, he carried them into the back room before returning to help. "So, Dad, how's business been?"

"Great, actually. I've got some additional shelving coming and we're expanding again." When the store first opened, there was extra space behind the sales floor that Sean didn't need. Over the last few years as business expanded, Sean had gradually extended the store into the empty space. "I'm hoping the shelving will be here right after we return, and I can get the new area set up."

The front door opened and Bobby saw Sam walk into the store, led by an interesting dog on a leash. Sean smiled. "Hi, Chloe," he said, and the dog's tail began wagging vigorously. Sam unhooked the leash and the dog raced to Sean, immediately rolling over, wanting her belly scratched.

Bobby stared at Sean. "New addition?"

"Yeah. We just got her a week ago. A customer who runs a dog rescue organization asked us about taking her. She's really well-behaved. We think she's part boxer and part bull terrier, but we don't know for sure." Sean continued rubbing her belly as she lolled on the floor. "She's just as sweet as can be." He stood up and she whirled around and began wandering through the store.

"You didn't tell me you'd gotten a dog." Bobby knelt and held out his hand. Chloe walked up to him gingerly, sniffed his hand, and then darted away.

"It happened rather quickly," Sean said, stroking her coat as she passed. "She's a little shy, but she loves it in the store and the customers seem to love her too. Since she's been here, we've had a marked increase in the number of customers with dogs." After making her rounds of the store, Chloe settled on a cushion in the corner.

Sam approached and gave Sean a kiss before engulfing Bobby in a big hug. "Thank you for doing this."

Bobby returned the hug. "Doing what, minding the store?" he asked. Sam nodded as he released Bobby from his grip. "I'm thrilled to do it. The two of you deserve a vacation. When do you leave, anyway?"

"Tomorrow morning. We're flying to Puerto Rico and staying at a resort hotel for the night. Then we're boarding a ship for a seven-day cruise."

Bobby was confused, but Sean interrupted with an explanation. "At first we were going to spend the week on an island, but Sam surprised me with the cruise." It looked to Bobby like the surprise was a big hit. He couldn't remember the last time he'd seen Dad this excited about something that didn't involve either Kenny or himself. In that split second, it occurred to him just how much Sean and Sam had done for both of them, how much they'd given up to make sure he and Kenny had whatever they needed.

"When's Kenny supposed to be here?" Bobby asked as he began opening the cases on the trolley and filling the displays.

"I expect him any time," Sean said. He just couldn't stand in one place for more than two seconds.

Bobby finished with one of the cases, breaking down the box and starting on another as he watched his dad pacing off his nervous energy. Finally, Sean wandered off to help a customer.

"He's been like this for days," Sam chuckled as he helped Bobby. "I'm so glad we're doing this."

"So, I know you're leaving out of Puerto Rico. What other islands are you visiting?"

"We stop in Aruba, Curacao, St. Maarten, and St. Thomas. I've already got us booked on a snorkeling trip in Aruba and a WaveRunner excursion on St. Thomas." Sam leaned close, a wicked look on his face. "I know I shouldn't tell you this," he said, his eyes flicking to Sean, "but I also booked a special excursion to Ocean Beach on the French side of St. Maarten."

Bobby elbowed Sam conspiratorially and said, "I take it it's clothing-optional." Sam nodded slightly and Bobby made a zipper motion on his lips. "Sounds to me like you're both really excited."

They finished filling the displays and Bobby broke down the rest of the boxes, hauling them and the trolley to the back. After a quick trip to the restroom, he wandered through the back. The table he and Kenny used to do their homework on was gone, the space now part of the enlarged sales floor. He found himself smiling as he wandered into the office. Maybe a trip home was just what he needed. Sitting down in the desk chair, he pulled out a sketchpad and began to draw.

KENNY pulled his car into one of the parking spaces in front of the store. Turning off the engine, he got out and wandered inside, only to be met with a chorus of greetings and a plethora of hugs. After talking to everyone, he wandered to the back looking for Bobby. He found him in the office, his face in a sketchbook. Standing quietly in the doorway, Kenny watched as Bobby's delicate hands skipped over the page, his pencil lightly scraping the paper. The man was beautiful like this. No stress, no worry, just relaxed concentration— Bobby's senses completely attuned to what he was doing. Kenny knew from experience that the world could fall around him and Bobby would notice nothing. He knocked on the door frame to get his attention.

Bobby looked up from his drawing and smiled. Kenny loved that smile. He hadn't seen it much in the past few years, but there it was, though it faded quickly. "Kenny." Bobby got up and hugged him perfunctorily. Even so, Kenny couldn't help thinking how good the man felt in his arms. Until they left for college, Kenny had been the smaller of the two, but during his freshman year, he shot up, and his intense physical training had bulked him up considerably. He was now taller and broader, and he outweighed Bobby by a good fifty pounds.

"It's so good to see you," Bobby said, looking up at him. Kenny had to stop himself from doing what he wanted to do. Bobby's lips looked so full and kissable, and the shine in those expressive eyes drew him in. Then the cold look he'd come to expect passed over Bobby's face and the moment passed.

"It's good to see you too," Kenny said as Bobby settled back in the chair. "How's school?"

"Really good. Just one term and a senior project to go. Some of the professors have encouraged me to go on to graduate school right away, but I haven't decided."

"Have you decided on your project?" Kenny saw a bit of the light in Bobby's eyes dim.

"Not yet. Because of my past work, there's a lot of pressure. I think they're looking for some impressive piece, but I can't get inspired. All my ideas basically suck. How about you?" Their conversation seemed casual, but underlying it was a tension Kenny wished he could sweep away.

"One last term and the police academy in the fall." Kenny's response was matter-of-fact, clearly devoid of excitement.

Bobby had put his feet on the desk but dropped them with a thud. "What's wrong?"

"It isn't quite what I expected it to be, I guess. I've been accepted to the academy and all, but I'm not sure it's what I want." He'd been having doubts for a while, but they seemed to be intensifying the closer he got to graduation. "Maybe I just need a rest and some time away."

Bobby's head nodded absently. "Probably."

Kenny watched as Bobby went back to his sketch, immersing himself in his drawing. Not wanting to disturb him, he began to get up. "Please don't move," Bobby said. Kenny settled back in the chair as Bobby continued drawing, fingers and pencil gliding over the paper, his focus shifting to Kenny and then back to the paper.

After about fifteen minutes he saw Bobby smile and put down his pencil before holding up the pad for him to see. This was the first drawing that Bobby had done of him in years, and Kenny couldn't suppress a smile.

"Hey, boys." Sean walked into the office and sat down on the futon against the wall, Chloe jumping up next to him. Sam followed a few minutes later, sitting on the other side of his lover. "I need to go over a few things before tomorrow." Bobby closed his pad and put it on the desk as both of them focused their attention on Sean. "I've got plenty of stock, with an order coming in Wednesday, so you should be fine. If Sarah calls, take her order and call the distributor. The number's by the phone." He turned to Bobby. "You know what to do." Kenny saw Bobby nod, and they waited for Sean to continue. "Keep a sharp eye on the doors. In the last week or so, a couple cases of wine have gone missing, including a case of Bollinger." Sean looked to Sam, who continued.

"We've called it in and investigated but can't figure out where it went. The stockroom was locked and trash removal supervised." Sam put his arm around Sean's shoulders. "It's taken me three days to convince Sean not to cancel the trip because of this, so please keep a close watch on anyone in the back room. I don't think it's Jimmy, the kid who cleans up for Sean, because the night the Bollinger went missing, he wasn't even here."

Sean took over. "I think a customer somehow got into the back while we were busy, so please be careful."

Bobby looked to Kenny and then back to Sean and Sam. "You can count on us."

Kenny felt his jaw tighten as he ground his teeth together. The thought of someone stealing from Sean made him furious. "Absolutely."

Sean smiled and seemed to relax. "Thank you. We really appreciate both of you using your break to help out."

For Kenny, there was absolutely no question or hesitation about helping. He owed the two of them so much, and manning the store with Bobby for a week was small payment enough. Besides, maybe this was a chance for he and Bobby to reconnect again after so much time apart. "You guys just enjoy your vacation and don't worry about a thing," he said.

"Thank you," Sean said, getting up and hugging each of them before going back out to wait on customers. "Katie and Laura are closing tonight, so I made reservations for dinner. You might want to head to the house."

"I'll take Bobby back to the house, and we'll meet you there in about an hour," Kenny replied.

"Okay. We'll see you then."

Bobby picked up his sketchpad, put it in his bag, and began manhandling his luggage.

"Let me get that," Kenny said, grabbing the suitcase, carrying it through the store, and stowing it in the back of his car. "Let's go."

Bobby climbed in the passenger seat, and Kenny pulled out and drove them back to the house, where they unloaded their stuff and hauled it up to their rooms.

As Kenny threw his bag on the bed and began putting his things away, it seemed both familiar and strange to be back in his room again. It looked the same but didn't feel the same, like he'd somehow gone back in time. His pictures were still on the walls, and his dresser and furniture were still there, but they felt like they belonged in another time.

"Feels weird, doesn't it?" Bobby asked. He stood in the doorway, looking in the room as Kenny sat on the edge of the bed.

"Yeah."

Bobby walked in and sat next to Kenny. "The thought of someone stealing from Dad really frosts my ass, and I don't know about you, but I intend to find out who's doing it."

"But how can we find out anything if Sam hasn't?" Kenny asked. "He said he already investigated."

Bobby glared at Kenny. "Well, I plan to even if you aren't interested."

"I didn't say I wasn't interested." Kenny could feel his defenses rising. "I just meant that I didn't know what we could do."

Bobby humphed softly. "You know Sam. What's he going to do? Look for a few cases of wine or spend his time reassuring and comforting Dad?" Bobby waited for Kenny's answer, but didn't get one. "So are you in?" He phrased it almost like a dare.

"Yeah, I'm in." Kenny felt himself staring daggers at Bobby. "It certainly won't hurt for us to look into it. I don't think we'll find anything, but maybe we can stop it from happening again." Kenny saw Bobby looking back into his eyes, and his anger slipped away upon seeing the uncertain, maybe a little scared, look in Bobby's eyes.

"Boys, we're home." Sean's voice traveled up the stairs as the front door closed.

"We're up here." Bobby called, and Kenny felt the bed move as Bobby got up from the bed and went to his room, shutting the door to change for dinner.

LATER that evening Sean was waiting for Sam to clean up and join him.

"Do you really think this is a good idea?" Sam asked, walking into the bedroom, naked, and Sean smiled, lifting the covers for his husband. "Those two haven't spent much time together in years." Sam climbed between the sheets, and Sean curled close.

"I know, and it's not right," Sean said. "They were so close, and I want them to have the chance to be close again." Sean watched as Sam punched his pillow, settling on the bed.

"Do you know what happened?" Sam finally got comfortable.

"Not really, but I know whatever it was happened the first Christmas after they went to college. They were never the same after that visit."

"You're such a busybody," Sam scolded lightly as he turned off the light.

"I am not." Sean ran his hand along Sam's side, making him laugh and squirm away. "I just want them to remember what they meant to each other." Sean rested his head against Sam's chest. "If they don't do it now, they'll move away and continue to grow apart."

"You're just feeling sad because they're growing up."

"And you're not?" Sean asked. "They're the closest we'll ever have to children, and we only got to have them for a few short years. I'm going to miss them both."

"Me too." Sam embraced Sean, holding him close. "Do you remember that summer cookout when Bobby was sixteen?" he asked, and Sean smiled, kissing his lover's skin, nodding as he did so. "And that trip to New York?"

"I do and I wish they were that age again." Sean sighed as he listened to the quiet house and the beat of Sam's heart.

CHAPTER 3

Six years ago

"BOBBY would you carry the potato salad?" Bobby watched as Sean picked up two bowls and headed for the back door, pushing it open with his foot.

"Sure, Dad, I've got it." Bobby came up behind him, holding the door as he stepped out onto the deck. They set their bowls on the table beneath the large red umbrella, and Bobby snagged a carrot from the vegetable tray. "Have you done this before?"

"No, this is my first big party." Sean looked around the deck. "I'm thinking of making this an annual event." The deck had tables and chairs shaded by brightly colored umbrellas, and the lawn had a number of chairs set in the shade, just waiting for their guests. The grill had been relocated out of the way to a spot near the garage. The weather had cooperated, and it was one of those rare Milwaukee summer days, warm but with little humidity. They usually got one or two a year.

Sam came out the back door, carrying the last of the dishes that had been sitting on the kitchen table. "It looks like our guests are starting to arrive." Bobby hurried to the edge of the deck to see who it was.

Mark and Tyler approached the deck on the side of the house. Sean greeted them, both he and Sam receiving a hug from each of them before Bobby felt himself engulfed in a pair of arms. "How are you doing, Bobby?" Mark asked, his hands slipping away.

"I'm good." Bobby stepped back and smiled. He just couldn't contain his excitement as he tugged Mark into the yard. They began talking art, with Bobby completely oblivious to everyone and everything around him.

"I have a show coming up in New York, and I was wondering if you'd like to go with me."

"New York?" Bobby beamed. "You want me to go to New York with you?" He could barely believe it. He was going to get to go to New York, to a gallery opening! He'd never done anything like that before and the excitement was almost too much for him. "I have to ask my dad. What's it like?" To Bobby, New York was somewhere he'd imagined as sort of a magical place with all these buildings and sights he'd heard about but never got to see. Mark told Bobby all about New York and all the things he could see.

Bobby looked toward the deck and saw Sean and Sam talking to Katie and Tyler, and they seemed really excited about something, almost as excited as Bobby was. Then he saw Katie extend her hand and wave something at Sean. "Looks like Katie's got big news," Mark quipped as he looked on as well. "We should go see what's going on, and you can ask your dad about New York."

Bobby ran across the yard, his excitement too much for him to contain. "Dad!" he called as he jumped on the deck, skidding to a stop in front of Sean. "Mark just told me that he has a show in New York next month, and he asked if I could go along with him." Bobby beamed with excitement. "Can I go with him?"

"Well," Sean began, his expression not looking very promising, "I don't know."

"Dad, please." Bobby wasn't above pleading. A real art opening in New York—this was like a dream for him.

"Mark told us about it last week, and we're all going. It'll be our summer vacation." Sean smiled, and Bobby let out a whoop.

Most of the party conversations stopped for a second before resuming.

"You mean it?" Bobby could hardly believe it.

"Yes, I mean it. You can take a friend along as well."

Bobby hugged Sean, holding tight to the one person who'd shown him love and kindness, who always seemed to know what he needed or wanted, and who did his best to give it to him.

"I thought you couldn't leave the store," Sam said to Sean.

"I'll figure something out. This will be great for Bobby." Sean's smile was huge as he looked at Bobby, and Bobby could tell his dad was almost as happy about going as Sam was.

Katie smirked next to Sean. "Laura and I can manage for a week while you're on vacation." She turned her eyes to the sky, shaking her head. "Sheesh."

"Sam, Sean." The gate to the deck opened, and Sam's partner on the police force joined the party.

"Hey, Ron. I'm glad you could come." Bobby watched the two men shake hands, but Bobby craned his head, hoping that Ron wasn't alone. Then he saw the person he was looking for, and he ran to meet him.

"Kenny! I was hoping you'd be able to come." Kenny and Bobby were in some of the same classes and had met in school, becoming fast friends.

"Me too, but Dad thought he might have to work. I guess he traded shifts or something." Bobby led Kenny to the cooler, and they each grabbed a soda. Kenny popped open the top of his and sipped, both boys looking around the yard.

"You wanna throw the football until it's time to eat?" Bobby felt nervous and wanted his friend to have a good time.

"Sounds good." Kenny kept sipping his soda.

"I'll be right back." Bobby raced into the garage and got his ball. Then they moved to an unused portion of the yard and began throwing the ball back and forth for a while until they got tired of it. He'd never really had many friends, other than Steve from the deli down the street from Sean's store, and he wanted to make a good impression on Kenny. Bobby tried to think of something else to do. "You wanna play video games?" he asked, figuring that was a winner since Ron wouldn't let him get one of his own.

"Cool." The smile on Kenny's face told him that was a hit.

They went inside and up to Bobby's room. Bobby turned on the console, and they picked out a game. Sitting on the edge of the bed, they began shooting aliens. "So what's going on?" Bobby twisted his body and shot, catching a ray-toting alien in the chest. "You've been acting funny all afternoon." He kept shooting even after Kenny stopped and put down his controller.

"I've got something on my mind. Okay?" Kenny sounded a little scared.

"Okay, you don't have to be mean about it. I was just askin'." The game ended, and Bobby set down his controller. Turning to face Kenny, he waited for his friend to explain what was going on.

"You wanna play or talk?" Kenny asked. Something was definitely bothering him. Kenny rarely got snippy with anyone. It just wasn't in his nature.

"You've obviously got something on your mind, so you may as well tell me or else I'll have to tickle it out of you." Bobby jumped onto Kenny, fingers rubbing along his ribs as they giggled wildly, and Kenny tried to thrash Bobby off him. This was a game they played quite often, one Bobby rarely lost. "So tell me what's got your underwear in a twist, and I'll stop."

"Bobby!" The tickling continued until Kenny panted his surrender. "Bobby!"

The tickling stopped, and Bobby waited for his friend to finally tell him what was up.

"Bobby, I'm gay."

"Well, duh, tell me something I didn't already know." Bobby picked up a pillow and hit Kenny across the head, the laughter starting again as Kenny took the other pillow and began swatting Bobby with it until they ran out of steam and flopped down on the bed.

"How did you know about me? Am I a real flamer or something?" The look on his face was so earnest that Bobby had to stifle a laugh. But he failed miserably and ended up on the bed in a fit of giggles.

"No, you're not a flamer. I could tell because I'm gay, and we just know each other somehow. I don't know how it works, but it does. Not that it really matters." Bobby controlled his laughter and sat on the bed. Kenny looked miserable. "What's the problem? There are plenty of gay kids in school. It's really no big deal."

"*They* don't have to tell my dad." Kenny suddenly looked miserable, and Bobby pulled him into a hug trying to comfort his friend.

"Sam says that your dad's pretty cool. He used to have a problem with gays, but he's been partners with Sam for years. I don't think you have anything to worry about."

"There's a big difference between having a gay partner on the force and your son telling you he's gay. I just don't know how Dad's going to react." Kenny began chewing on his lip—a trait that always told Bobby that his friend was really upset. "How long have you known you were gay?"

"Geez, like since I was thirteen. You've known since then too, haven't you?" Kenny nodded and looked down at the floor. "It's cool. I won't say anything, but you should tell your dad."

"Bobby!" The voice calling up the stairs was familiar and made him smile.

"Grandma and Grandpa are here." Bobby got up off the bed and straightened up. "It's okay, I won't say anything. I promise." Kenny got up as well, and they started for the door. "Oh, before I forget, we're going to New York next month, and Dad said that I could take a friend with me. You wanna go?"

That brought a smile to Kenny's face. "I'll have to ask my dad."

"I'll ask Dad and Sam to ask him. That way it'll be harder for him to say no." Bobby knew from experience that Ron usually said no first, where Sean usually tried to say yes if he could. They left the room and headed down the stairs.

Back on the deck, Bobby was hugged and kissed by his grandmother. "You remember my friend Kenny?" Bobby said during a break in the affection.

"Of course." Sean's mother smiled.

"I'd hug you, but you'd probably think that I'm a little young for you." It was Kenny's offhand way of asking for a hug too. Her smile shifted to a grin when Kenny made up his own mind and went ahead and hugged her anyway.

"We all need hugs, young man, no matter how old we are."

Kenny straightened up, "Yes, ma'am." Kenny stepped back and looked around to see if he'd somehow blown his teenage rep, but no one was paying attention, so he was safe.

"Son." Bobby turned and saw Sean approaching. "I was wondering if you and Kenny would be willing to help Sam with the grilling." The boys looked at each other and smiled before taking off toward the garage.

KENNY practically shook with excitement. His dad had given permission for him to go to New York. He could hardly believe it—

New York with Bobby and his family. How cool was that? He'd never been away from home for that long, and there were so many things he was going to get to see. But the best part was that he'd get to spend a whole week with his best friend. "Kenny, we need to get home," Ron said as he approached where he and Bobby were sitting on the grass and making plans for their trip. Kenny looked up at his dad. "Okay, but can I have five more minutes?"

"Sure, five minutes." Ron smiled indulgently and rejoined Sean and Sam on the deck.

"I can't believe he said yes."

Bobby grinned as he picked at the grass. "I told you Dad would get him to say yes."

Kenny got up and looked at his watch. "I'll call you tomorrow." Bobby jumped to his feet, and Kenny found himself pulled into a hug. "Okay, I gotta go." Kenny wasn't sure how to react to Bobby's affection. Part of him wanted to hug back, but another part tried to hold him in check because he had to play it cool. He settled on making his friend happy and returned Bobby's hug before backing away and joining his dad on the deck.

"Ready to go?" Ron was already saying his goodbyes, and Kenny did the same, following his dad through the other guests and out to the front where their bikes were parked.

Ron had figured he'd have a beer or two, so they'd ridden their bicycles to the party. Kenny loved it. Bike riding was one of the things they did together. "Hey, Dad, race you home!" Kenny put on his helmet, pushed back the kickstand, hopped on his bike, and took off, laughing as he called back, "Getting old?"

He heard Ron shout back as he began pedaling. "I'll show you old!"

Kenny laughed and put his head down, pedaling down the streets as fast as his legs would pedal. "Gotta be faster if you wanna win," Kenny heard Ron call over as he pulled level with him. He beat his feet to the pedals, giving it everything he had as they turned the corner to their street, and Kenny reached the front of the house just ahead of his father.

Kenny braked to a stop and threw his arms in the air. "I won!" He looked over at Ron and saw his father's bright smile.

"Yes, you did." Ron never let him win at anything. Whenever they played games, his dad played to win—even when Kenny was younger—so this was sweet and a real victory. "I knew you'd beat me soon." Kenny took off his helmet, and Ron ruffled his hair before they began walking their bikes through the yard to the garage. He was so lucky. His dad was great; they did things together and spent time together. It was so cool. Kenny heard the kids at school talking about how their dads spent most of their time drinking or watching television. Kenny knew how good he had it. He just wished he could figure out how to tell his dad... but he couldn't, not now.

"What's got you so quiet all of a sudden? I thought you'd be crowing about your victory."

"I'm fine, just thinking." Kenny waited while Ron hung the bikes from the garage rafters before following him back toward the back door. "Thank you for letting me go on vacation with Bobby." He didn't know what else to say, and his imposed silence was going to make Ron wonder.

"You're welcome." Ron unlocked the door, and Kenny headed right up to his room. He immediately opened his closet. He was so excited and ready to start packing now, even though they weren't leaving for a month.

Kenny had friends, but no one else was like Bobby. There was no one else he could tell his deepest, darkest secret and know it would be okay. Bobby wouldn't reject him. In fact, he doubted there was anything Bobby wouldn't see him through. If Kenny were honest, he had to admit he was a little in awe of his friend. Bobby was super-talented, and there were times when he'd been jealous of him. But that hadn't lasted long. Bobby was so good to him. He was the best friend Kenny had ever had, and he couldn't imagine a better one. The phone rang, and Kenny heard his dad answer it and then call to him. He raced down the stairs and picked up the receiver. "Hey, Bobby."

"Dad told me he needs some help at the store. Would you like to go in with us? Dad said we could earn some money for the trip."

"Let me ask." This was just like Bobby, always looking out for him too. "Dad, it's Bobby. His dad needs help at the store, and he said that we could earn some money for the trip." Even though it was work, he and Bobby always enjoyed working at the store.

He saw Ron smile as he looked up from the television. "Sure, what time?"

Bobby obviously heard, because he answered right away. "We'll pick you up at eight-thirty." Kenny said goodbye and hung up, telling Ron what the plans were before joining him in the living room. He and Bobby had been friends since Bobby first came to school, but over the last few months, they'd grown closer and closer. After today, Kenny really understood why. They were both different, both gay. But there was more. Kenny thought Bobby was the most talented person in the world. Whenever someone at school threatened either of them, it was Bobby who took them on.

"You've been quiet since we got home. Is something wrong?" Ron sounded concerned.

Kenny screwed up his courage. "I wanted to tell you something." Yes, he could do this. It was on the tip of his tongue to tell him everything, but a high-pitched beeping cut him off.

Ron was on his feet and dialing the phone before he could say anything else. Kenny released his held breath and waited until he heard the phone being returned to its cradle. "I have to go in, they need help. I'll probably be gone most of the night." This happened sometimes and Kenny knew the drill. "We'll talk when I get home." Ron said goodbye and gave him a hug. A few minutes later, Kenny heard the back door close as his dad raced to his car.

The house was quiet as Kenny made sure all the doors were locked. He was just about to go upstairs when the phone rang. It was Bobby, wondering if he wanted to come over. "I'm okay. I'll see you in the morning," Kenny said, and he hung up the phone and climbed the stairs. After getting cleaned up, he climbed into bed, listening to every noise in the house. After an hour of worrying and waiting, he wished he'd taken Bobby up on his offer. This was nothing new. He always worried when his dad was out late or got special calls. It was one of the hardships of having a police officer for a father, but Ron loved it, and he was proud of his father, proud that Ron was a good cop. But if anything ever happened to Ron, Kenny didn't know what he'd do. Eighteen months ago, his dad had been hurt on the job, not badly, but it had scared Kenny half to death.

He must have fallen to sleep, because sometime in the night, he woke as the back door opened and closed. Then he heard familiar footsteps in the house and the refrigerator door open and close. Dad was home. That thought was enough to relax him, and he didn't even hear the footsteps on the stairs or see his door open as his dad checked on him before going to bed. Dad was safe, his world was secure, and he was asleep.

CHAPTER 4

"BOYS, you need to go to sleep. We're going to be up early in the morning."

Bobby watched as Sean turned off the light. "Okay, Dad." Bobby settled in his bed, trying to get comfortable. Kenny was sleeping on an air mattress on the floor. "We're going to have so much fun. Dad says that after New York, we're going to the beach, some place called Cape May. Mark and Tyler borrowed a place there from a friend."

"Are they coming along too?"

"Mark's meeting us in New York, and he'll ride with us to Cape May where we'll all meet up with Tyler. Dad told me the ocean beaches are really different from the beaches we have around here."

"Boys, go to sleep."

"'Night, Kenny." Bobby lay down and closed his eyes, trying his best to fall asleep.

He'd just fallen to sleep when he felt someone shaking him. "Bobby, it's time to get up."

"What time is it?" Bobby yawned wide, not even trying to cover it.

"Five-thirty. You boys need to get cleaned up and in the car in twenty minutes." Sean turned on the light and left the room.

"I'll go first if you want." Bobby got out of bed, straightened the covers, and got in the bathroom. He cleaned up in record time before returning to the bedroom. Kenny was already up and dressed. He took his turn in the bathroom, and they both rushed downstairs. Sam passed by as he carried things out to the SUV.

"Need some help?" Bobby offered

"I'm almost done. You boys go into the kitchen. Sean has breakfast ready for you." It was quite a production. The boys ate while the last things were packed. Sean made a final walk through the house, locked the door, and climbed into the passenger seat. They were on the road by six, the boys falling right back to sleep.

Bobby woke up to the sound and feel of a moving vehicle. "Where are we?" He sat up, rubbing his eyes, and saw flat fields and farmhouses passing outside the windows. Kenny was leaning against him, arms holding him tight, still asleep, and Bobby tried his best not to move so he didn't wake him.

"Indiana," Sam said. "The two of you slept for a while." A soft snore carried from the passenger seat. "Maybe I should say the three of you." Sam smiled from the driver's seat at his snoring lover.

Sam drove as long as he could but eventually pulled into a rest area for a pit stop. As soon as the vehicle stopped, Sean and Kenny woke up, and everyone piled out for a much-needed stretch before piling back in and continuing down the road. Sean took over driving and Sam opened the cooler, passing out food and drinks.

They played traveling games across Ohio, where they also stopped for lunch. In Pennsylvania, they watched as forested mountains and river valleys passed outside the windows. By the time they hit New Jersey, it was dark, but they were almost there, and Sam pulled up in front of their New York hotel at just after nine. Sean checked them in while Sam and the boys unloaded the luggage before the valet took the vehicle. The exhausted group took the elevator to their floor, and Sean unlocked the small, two-bedroom hotel suite. Within an hour, everyone was fast asleep.

Bobby woke in the middle of the night to a strange sensation. For one thing, he wasn't alone in bed and the person with him was holding him tight. It took him a second to realize it was Kenny. It took him another split second to realize that he liked it.

"I'm sorry," Kenny mumbled softly as his arm retreated.

Kenny rolled away, but Bobby rolled to meet him, putting his arms protectively around his best friend, returning the comfort he'd received. "Nothing to be sorry for." They both went right back to sleep.

"MORNING, boys."

Bobby rolled away from Kenny as Sean entered their room. "Daaaad." Bobby pulled the covers up to block the light. "You're way too perky in the morning."

"I am not perky! And if you want breakfast, you better move before they close." Bobby heard the annoyance in Sean's voice, and he winced involuntarily.

"Sorry, Dad." He wasn't sure if Sean was serious or not, but then he smiled, and Bobby knew he was kidding.

"Just get yourself some breakfast. We're catching the subway so we can go to the Statue of Liberty."

"Okay," Both boys said together as they started getting out of bed.

"Your dad's pretty cool, you know that?" Kenny grabbed his stuff and padded toward the bathroom.

Bobby started pulling off his pajamas before rummaging in his suitcase, looking for the clothes he wanted to wear, coming up with a pair of jeans and one of Sean's old T-shirts. "I know," he said. "It's just hard sometimes." Bobby had told Kenny about the foster homes and his time on the street a while ago, and he was often surprised at how perceptive his friend was when it came to other people's feelings.

Kenny stuck his head out the bathroom door, his mouth full of toothpaste. "'Cause you think they might not love you any more if you do something wrong?" It came out sort of garbled, but Bobby understood.

"Yeah, sometimes, I guess." He heard Kenny spit in the sink, followed by the sound of running water.

"You know that's never gonna happen. You could murder someone, and your dad and Sam would stick by ya." The bathroom door closed and soon he heard the shower start.

Bobby got his things ready, and when Kenny emerged, he hightailed it into the bathroom so he could clean up and take his own shower. When he left the bathroom in his underwear, Kenny was dressed, sitting on the side of the bed, biting on one of his fingernails. "What's bothering you?" Bobby asked.

"Nothin'."

Bobby pulled on his jeans and the vintage shirt he'd borrowed permanently from Sean. "Something is, 'cause you only bite your nails when you're nervous. So spill it."

"Do you think Sean and Sam know about me?"

Bobby shrugged. "Doesn't matter if they do. They'd never say anything. But since Dad saw me cuddling you this morning, I bet they do."

"Oh." Kenny looked at the floor, his fingers going to his mouth.

"You wanna talk to them about it?" Bobby had no doubt that either Sean or Sam would talk to Kenny and answer any questions he had. God knows they'd talked to him enough about it. Not that that was a bad thing, just embarrassing. Bobby smiled to himself remembering when Sean turned three shades of red while he was telling him about sex and condoms and stuff. "I know they'll listen." Kenny shook his head and blushed brightly.

"I just don't know how I'm gonna tell my dad." Bobby sat down next to his friend, hugging him close. "I almost did a while ago but chickened out."

"You're the best friend I ever had. When you're ready, I'll come with you."

"You will?"

"Sure I will. But not today. We need to get ready for some fun. We're going to the Statue of Liberty, and tonight we get to go to a fancy gallery opening." They both smiled and began pulling on their shoes, rushing so they wouldn't miss breakfast. The nerves and angst were forgotten, at least temporarily, with the prospect of fun.

THE gallery was hopping by the time they arrived. On the ride over, they'd talked and laughed, but as soon as they entered, Bobby became hushed, almost reverent.

"You two look around, but don't leave the gallery." Sean said before he and Sam began to look around.

Both boys nodded, and Sam and Sean made their way through the crowd while Bobby led Kenny to the start of the exhibition. Kenny turned to Bobby. "I don't understand this very well."

Bobby's arm went around Kenny's shoulder. "I'll explain things as we go." They started at the beginning and walked through the exhibit with Kenny asking Bobby questions. "The good thing is that art is all about what the work means to you. The rest of it's just a bunch of bunk and art-speak. When you look at each piece, ask yourself what you see and how it makes you feel or what it makes you think of." They were standing in front of one of Mark's pieces. "See, this is a portrait of someone we don't know and will probably never know, but what do you see in the expression?"

Kenny looked at the painting for a while, "Anger, resentment. The guy looks like he's mean and not too bright." Kenny leaned close to read the card. "Says it's a portrait of a guy named Rush Limbaugh. What does the red dot over the price mean?"

"Probably that it's sold." They moved on and continued around a corner, Bobby stopping in his tracks.

"Bobby," Kenny said, pointing. "That's you." Kenny read the tag, "It says 'portrait of a young artist'." Kenny stepped back, standing next to Bobby. "Wow. Did you know?" Bobby shook his head, almost unable to believe what he was seeing. "The tag says 'not for sale'."

"I see you like your portrait." Bobby recognized Mark's voice and nodded. "I wasn't sure it would be done in time, but I got it finished."

"I'm glad you're not selling it." For some reason he didn't want a stranger owning it.

Mark broke into a big smile. "I can't. It isn't mine to sell—it's yours."

Bobby could hardly believe his ears. "Really?" Mark nodded as Bobby gave him a huge hug, and Sean and Sam joined the group. "Did you know?" Both Sean and Sam smiled and nodded as Bobby watched them, still hugging Mark. Bobby released Mark and stood looking at his portrait, not even realizing he was gripping Kenny's hand in his or seeing the warm look that passed between Sam and Sean.

"We should see the rest of the exhibition," Sean said, placing a hand on Bobby's shoulder as Mark was pulled away by one of the show's patrons.

Bobby tore his eyes away from his own likeness. "Okay, Dad." And they continued through the gallery, viewing the rest of the show, with Mark rejoining them toward the end.

"The gallery is providing me transportation back to the hotel in a few minutes, so you can ride with me instead of taking a taxi."

Mark led them outside, and a black limousine pulled up to the curb, where the chauffeur opened the door. "That's our ride," Mark said with a smile as the boys looked at each other with stunned grins before hopping in and settling on the seat, the adults following behind.

"I didn't have a chance to give you this earlier." Mark handed Kenny a package in plain brown paper. "I did this for you after the cookout last month."

Kenny ripped the paper and looked at the drawing. "Thank you." He turned it around and showed everyone a pen and ink drawing of himself and his father, matted and framed.

"You're welcome. I'll have it shipped home with Bobby's piece so you won't have to carry it for the rest of the trip." Bobby looked over and watched as Kenny's eyes gleamed. Then he saw his friend hug the stuffing out of Mark.

The limousine stopped at the hotel, and they piled out, walking through the lobby to the elevators and riding up to their floor in tired silence. In the suite, Kenny turned on the television, and Bobby went into the bedroom.

"Are you having a fun time?" Sean asked, sitting on the edge of the bed. Bobby turned and sat next to him.

"Yeah, I think we both are." Bobby looked through the open doorway to where Kenny sat in the living room. "Is it wrong for me to wish that Kenny was my brother? 'Cause I wish he was and that we could live together all the time." He was going to miss having Kenny around when their vacation was over.

Sean smiled. "No, it's not wrong. But you might not get along as well if you lived together."

"I know, but I still wish he was my brother sometimes."

"That's a very good thing," Sean said. "A lot of people never have the kind of friendship you and Kenny have." He stood and left the room just as Kenny entered, jumping onto the bed.

"Did your dad say what we're doing tomorrow?" he asked. Bobby shook his head. "I'm sure it'll be fun." Bobby found himself pushed back on the bed, pillows began flying, and they both started giggling as the pillow fight turned into a tickle fight. Having a best friend was the greatest thing ever.

CHAPTER 5

BOBBY'S phone rang just as he was getting home from school, "Dad" flashing across the screen.

"How was your day?"

"It was good, Dad. I'm just glad the first week's over." He put his book bag in his room while he talked.

"Do you have homework you need help with?" Bobby rarely needed help any more, but Sean always asked anyway.

Bobby smiled into the phone. "Nope. I got most of it done, even the math. I was wondering if I could go over to Kenny's. He said his dad's working, and he asked if I could hang out."

"Okay, but you have work at the store you promised to get done."

"I know." Bobby moved through the house, heading to the kitchen for a snack. "I was planning to go in with you in the morning to organize the stockroom for you. Is that okay?"

Sean laughed into the phone. "Sure. Go hang out with Kenny."

"I'll have my phone if you need anything." Bobby opened the refrigerator and pulled out a soda. "Thanks, Dad."

"No problem. I should be home by nine, so don't be out too late."

"I won't. Maybe we'll come back and watch a movie with you." Bobby popped open the can and drank it down in a few gulps before tossing it into the recycling bin. "I'll see you later." He disconnected the call and pulled on a jacket before locking the house. Getting on his bike, he pedaled down the sidewalk.

Fifteen minutes later, he arrived at Kenny's, kicking down the stand and walking to the front door, which opened as he approached. "Kenny, what's wrong?" Bobby hurried inside and Kenny closed the door. "What's going on? You look scared as shit."

Kenny led him into the living room where the television was tuned to the news. "There's a robbery in progress, and I thought I saw Dad on the footage." Bobby knew what Kenny was feeling. He and Sean had waited up many times for Sam to come home after they'd seen something on the news. Now if Sam knew something was going on, he'd text them both just to let them know he was okay. Bobby fished around in his pocket and pulled out his phone. No message.

"They're probably okay. Let's watch something else, and we'll wait together."

"Okay, what'd you like to watch?" Kenny handed Bobby the remote, found a *Star Trek: The Next Generation* rerun, and they both settled down to watch. "I haven't seen this one." During the first commercial, Kenny got a bag of chips, and they munched as they became engrossed in the episode.

Just as the episode finished, Bobby's phone buzzed with a message. "IM OK, YOU AT KENNYS."

Bobby replied, "YES," and sent the message. "Sam just sent his okay message." Kenny relaxed as another episode started. "You wanna order a pizza?"

"Sure, I'll call it in." Kenny got up and placed the order. "They'll be here in half an hour." Kenny flopped onto the sofa, pulling a handful of chips out of the bag as they watched.

The second episode was almost over when the doorbell rang. Kenny got up and answered the door but didn't return right away. "Kenny, you got enough money?" Bobby didn't get a response, so he walked into the hall. Kenny was leaning against a wall; Sam and another police officer were standing in the doorway. "Sam, what happened?" Bobby stood next to Kenny, putting an arm around his friend.

"Kenny," Sam said, stepping forward, "your dad's been shot."

A look of utter disbelief covered Kenny's face. "Is he going to be okay?" His voice was so soft that Bobby could barely hear it standing right next to him.

"We don't know. We came to take you to the hospital." Kenny nodded but didn't move, and Bobby thought he might fall over.

"Hello, did someone order a pizza?" The Domino's guy stood in the open doorway. The two police officers turned around, and Sam took some money from his wallet and paid him, taking the pizza.

"We should go. Bobby, head on home, Sean should be there in a little while." Sam took Kenny's arm and guided him through the door. Bobby followed behind them and got in the back seat of the cruiser, sitting next to Kenny. Sam looked into the back seat, and Bobby was prepared to argue that he was going too, but Sam kept quiet and started the car.

"It's gonna be okay," Bobby said, holding his friend. He felt Kenny's slight body shaking in fear and worry. "I'm sure he'll be fine." He continued the reassurance like a mantra as they barreled through intersections and flew down side streets. Kenny said nothing, which made Bobby even more nervous.

Approaching the hospital, they pulled into the emergency entrance, and Bobby waited while Sam jumped out, opening the back door for him and Kenny. "We'll be here a while. I'll call Sean and have him join us," Sam said. The other officer nodded and pulled away as soon as the door closed.

Sam led them inside and spoke to someone at the desk, while Bobby held Kenny close and waited. "They brought your dad in less than an hour ago. He's in one of the private examining rooms," Sam said, and the woman from the desk led them down a hallway and into a room with glass walls.

As soon as Kenny saw Ron, he raced through the door and to his bedside. "Dad! Dad!" The room was full of equipment and monitors: one beeping with every heartbeat and another with a bellows that rose and fell as well as a bunch of other things that made noise. A hook on the wall held a deep red bag and another one that was nearly clear. "Dad, wake up." Kenny touched Ron's hand, tears running down his face. "Please open your eyes, Dad." Kenny began crying, his head bowing to his father's hand, his small body shuddering as he sobbed. "Please, Dad."

A woman came in and changed out one of the IV bags. "We need to prep him for surgery." Bobby looked up at her and saw her soft expression.

Sam put his hand on Kenny's shoulder. "We need to go." Sam helped Kenny up, and Bobby hugged him as soon as he stepped away from Ron. Walking slowly, he led Kenny out of the room, but the teenager turned and stopped in the hall across from the room, watching as nurses worked on Ron. "Kenny," Sam coaxed, but Kenny was having none of it. He watched as they prepped, and he watched as they wheeled the gurney out of the room. The nurse and orderlies stopped in the hall to let Kenny touch his dad's hand. Kenny watched until they turned the corner at the end of the hall. Then and only then would he allow himself to be ushered away.

KENNY saw Sean when he, Bobby, and Sam arrived in the waiting area. Kenny flopped on the sofa and Bobby immediately sat next to him. Bobby held him almost protectively as they sat without saying a word for the longest time.

"What happened?" Kenny asked, wiping his eyes with the back of his hand, trying in vain to keep his eyes dry as he looked up at Sam.

"We were called to what we thought was a break-in, but we found ourselves in a drug house. They opened fire as we approached the house, and your dad got shot in the chest as he pushed me to the ground." Sam alternately looked from Kenny to Bobby to Sean and back to Kenny. "He saved my life." His voice trailed off as his lip trembled and left the rest unsaid.

Kenny watched as Sam, a police officer and one of the strongest men he'd ever known, besides Sean, began to shake as he tried to stave off the tears just below the surface. Sean got up and sat next to the man he loved most in the world. He stroked his arm as Sam tried to say more but couldn't, the words becoming choked in his throat. Kenny watched as Sam got up and began pacing the floor. Kenny almost joined him, but he couldn't leave Bobby's comforting embrace.

"Sam." He stopped walking at the sound of Sean's voice. "Why don't you go get us something to drink?" Sam nodded and slowly walked down the hall.

"What's going to happen?" Kenny could barely speak, there were so many things going on in his head. *What was going to happen to his dad? What was he going to do until his dad could come home?* He just couldn't get his head around anything except that complete, all-consuming worry.

"Once we hear from the doctor, we'll stop by the house, so you can get your things. You can stay with us for as long as you need."

"But, what if...?" The tears started again and he made no move to stop them.

"For as long as you need or want," Sean said, taking Kenny's hand in his and holding it until Sam returned with some sodas and coffee. Absently, they each took a cup and began to sip their drinks, none of them really tasting anything. Kenny knew he certainly wasn't.

They all turned their heads as they heard very determined footsteps approaching. "Chief," Sam said, and he tried to get up, but the man shook his head, and Sam settled back on the sofa. If he was surprised at the scene that greeted him, his face didn't register it.

"I just heard what happened and came right down. Is there anything I can do?"

"No," Sam answered, his voice stronger and more detached in the presence of the police chief. "They took him to surgery a little while ago. We may not hear anything for hours."

"I understand that Officer Johnson has a son."

"Yes." Sam indicated Kenny, and he began to stand up, but the chief motioned him to stay where he was. "He'll be staying with us," Sam continued.

The chief sat next to Kenny. "I've known your dad quite a while. I was his lieutenant when he first joined the force. He's a fine man and a fine officer."

Kenny nodded his head slowly. "Thank you, sir." He really didn't know what else to say, but it made him proud that the chief thought so much of his father, and he wiped his eyes again.

The chief turned his attention to Bobby, and Kenny gratefully settled back on the sofa. "Who's this fine young man?"

Sean answered this time. "Our son, Bobby."

The chief held out his hand, "It's good to meet you, son. I've heard you're quite an artist."

As the chief got up, Kenny saw a man approaching slowly, wearing scrubs and a very weary expression. All eyes turned to him, and Kenny watched as he slowly shook his head as he removed his cap. "The damage from the bullet was just too great. I'm sorry." The silence that followed was broken by a wail of grief from Kenny that filled the room and echoed down the hospital corridors. Gut-wrenching sobs just poured out of him.

Kenny clung to Bobby as his body heaved, tears streaming down his face, soaking the shoulder of Bobby's shirt. He felt Bobby's shoulders heaving beneath him, and he knew that Bobby was crying too. Then Bobby pulled away, and Sam pulled Kenny into his arms. He felt his body begin to move slowly, and Kenny realized that Sam was rocking him. Some primal, early instinct kicked in, and Kenny let himself be comforted. When he pulled back from Sam's embrace, he saw wet lines streaking the man's face. Other police officers began to arrive, and Kenny saw huge men in uniform wiping their eyes and turning away. It took awhile, but he began to get hold of himself, his tears subsiding, at least for now. Sam released him, and Kenny sat on the sofa, wiping his eyes, feeling dazed and confused.

Sam helped Kenny to his feet. "Let's go home." Everything else could wait at this point. Kenny felt Sam's arm around his shoulder and felt himself being guided toward the exit. He turned and saw Bobby and Sean following.

To say the drive to the house was somber was an understatement. The only sound was the occasional sniffle from the back seat.

In the house, Sean made them something light to eat that they all picked at. Kenny ate almost nothing, pushing back his chair and walking almost blindly into the living room. A few minutes later, the others joined him, Bobby sitting next to him on the sofa.

"What's going to happen to me?" Kenny asked as the tears began again.

Sam knelt next to him, an arm sliding protectively around his shoulder. "Your dad asked me a few months ago if I'd take care of you if anything happened to him. You'll have a home here for as long as you want one, so don't worry about that at all."

Kenny lifted his head slowly. "What's going to happen next?" He found he could barely talk around the lump in his throat.

"We need to make arrangements for the funeral and all that stuff." Sam shifted so Kenny could see him. "Sean and I—"

"Me too." Bobby interrupted, standing behind Sam.

"We're all here for you."

Kenny nodded, feeling lost and forlorn.

"Come on, Kenny, we should go to bed." Bobby held out his hand, and Kenny looked at it, not quite understanding what Bobby wanted. Then he slowly got up and let Bobby lead him off to bed.

"I've got some clothes you can borrow." Bobby opened the door to his room and guided him inside. Opening a drawer, he pulled out some sweatpants and a T-shirt, handing them to Kenny, who looked at them blankly. "Go get cleaned up."

Kenny nodded and shuffled off into the bathroom, returning a few minutes later changed and ready for bed. He sat on the edge of the bed—still feeling lost—while Bobby left the room. "Come on," Bobby said upon returning. He pulled back the covers, and they got into bed. As Kenny settled under the covers, Bobby wrapped his arms around his waist to hold him. Kenny felt the tears begin to well again, and to his relief, Bobby just held him and let him cry himself to sleep.

When Kenny was asleep, Bobby slowly got back up to use the bathroom and heard voices downstairs. He found Sam and Sean in the living room. "Is Kenny asleep?" Bobby nodded. "Thank God."

"Dad." Bobby sat next to Sean on the sofa. "I didn't mean it." He felt so guilty.

"Mean what?"

"When I wished that Kenny was my brother, I didn't mean for this to happen like this."

Sean smiled, hugging his son. "I know." Bobby heard Sean's voice hitch. "This didn't happen because of your wish."

"Then why?"

"People have been asking that question for thousands of years, and the answer is that no one knows. Bad things happen, good things happen, and we need to make the best of both. Today, Kenny lost his dad, but you both gained a brother." Bobby nodded. "He's going to need all of us right now."

Bobby nodded again. "I should go back to bed in case Kenny needs me." He climbed the stairs and found Kenny still asleep. Climbing into the bed, he felt Kenny shift and then settle again. Staring at the ceiling, he finally fell asleep.

KENNY, Bobby, Sam, and Sean arrived at the church for the funeral, Kenny hugging a framed drawing to his chest. Most of the pews were already full. Half the police force was there, along with many of Kenny's friends and teachers. The principal had closed the school so both faculty and students could attend the funeral. If it hadn't been for the reserved sign on one of the pews, they wouldn't have had a place to sit.

In the front of the church, a large picture of Kenny's dad in his uniform sat on an easel. As they walked to the front of the church, Kenny didn't stop at the pew but continued walking, climbing the steps to the altar. Lifting the photograph of his father, he set it aside and placed the drawing Mark had given him of Ron and him in its place. He heard a chorus of sniffles and soft sobs carry through the church, but he ignored them, trying to keep hold of himself. This was the way he wanted Ron remembered, not so much as a police officer, but as his father—the best father in the world. Taking a deep breath, Kenny turned and walked back to the pew, taking his seat next to Bobby.

The funeral itself was grand, with soaring music and a eulogy given by the Chief of Police. The flag-draped coffin was carried in and out by police officers in dress uniforms. Kenny sat stoically, almost detached through most of it, but he couldn't contain his tears when officers, friends, and members of the community told their stories of how much his father meant to them. The testimonies only accentuated his sense of loss, and he gave his grief free rein, letting it flow out of him.

When it was over, he felt Sam guiding him out of the pew to follow the coffin out of the church, and he watched as it was placed in the hearse before riding to the cemetery. Where the funeral had been a very public outpouring of grief, the cemetery was private. There was just the four of them, the minister, and the pall bearers. The minister said a few words, and one of the officers presented the flag to Kenny, who took it and instinctively hugged it to his chest. Kenny stepped forward, placing his hand on the casket, and said a few last words of goodbye, telling his dad how much he loved him and would miss him, before turning and walking alone toward the car.

LATE that afternoon, the four of them cleaned out the spare bedroom they'd been using as an office and made Kenny his own bedroom, moving in his bedroom furniture. "Where would you like to hang this?" Sean asked, handing Kenny the drawing of him and his dad.

"Over the bed." His voice sounded dull and listless, even to himself, but he really didn't care. Sean got the tools and hammered a hanger in the place he'd indicated and helped Kenny hang the drawing. When they were done, Kenny sat cross-legged on his bed, staring at it, wishing he could have one more day with his dad. "I never told him."

"Told him what?" Sean sat on the edge of the bed, looking at him.

"I never told him about me, about how I feel." He looked away from the picture and out the window. The tears started again, this time soft and slow. "He would have hated me for it."

"No, he wouldn't," Sean said. "He *knew*, Kenny. Your dad told me at the party this summer. It didn't matter to him, and he loved you. Never forget that. Your dad loved you, no matter what." Kenny moved to Sean and hugged him. This time the tears were slow and cleansing, a boy saying a final goodbye to the father he loved.

CHAPTER 6

BOBBY and Kenny walked into Sommelier Wines still carrying their books. "How's the Dynamic Duo?" Katie ribbed from behind the counter. "I'm starting to wonder if the two of you are joined at the hip." She smiled as she stepped away from the register to hug both boys before going back to work.

Sean emerged from the back room, wheeling cases of wine to the floor. "How was school?" He stopped near the display and began opening cases.

"Good," Bobby answered, "I've got an art project to finish up. I have to produce a drawing of an emotional vegetable." Bobby snickered.

Kenny laughed outright. "I suggested a cantankerous carrot or an egregious eggplant, but he turned me down." They all laughed.

Sean turned his attention to Kenny. "What do you have to do?"

"English," he sighed. "What else?" Kenny had been having a great deal of difficulty both in his sophomore grammar class and now in his composition class as a junior. "I have a five-hundred-word descriptive essay to write, and I have no idea where to start."

Bobby's hand went around his shoulders. "I'll help you, if you'll help me with math."

"That's a deal." They both headed to the back room to finish their homework.

"Don't forget, you both have chores and tomorrow's payday," Sean called as he went back to work.

"We won't." Both boys worked a few evenings a week and part of the weekend at the store, sweeping floors, filling shelves, and helping Sean with special events. But homework always came first, and in the six months Kenny had been living with them, his grades had improved immensely. Sean was like a mother hen, checking over both boys' homework on a nightly basis. Bobby didn't really need that level of help any longer, but Kenny did, so Sean checked both their work so that Kenny wouldn't feel singled out.

An hour later, they'd finished their homework, but books were still spread over the entire surface of the table in the back of the store.

"I don't know why I'm doing this. I'll never do well enough," Kenny said, looking up from the English grammar book he was studying.

"Of course you will. We're both going to do well on the SATs, and we're both going to get into college." His tone was so definite. Bobby knew that Kenny was trying his best. He hadn't been the best student, but there was no way Bobby was going to leave him behind. "We'll both get into college and we'll be roommates." For him, there was no question that he and his best friend, now brother, would always be together.

Kenny closed the book and put it on the table, shaking his head. "Bobby, no. I've decided that I'm going to be a police officer like my father. If I get into college, I'm going to become a police officer like my dad and Sam—and you," Kenny looked at Bobby very seriously, "you are going to be a great artist, and you're going to one of the world's finest art schools. I can't go with you, and I won't allow you to sell yourself short because of me."

"I won't be selling myself short—"

"Yes, you will. You deserve the best, most talented teachers and the brightest students in a place where creativity is encouraged. As my brother and my best friend, I want that for you."

Bobby had never thought that he and Kenny would go to different schools, and the notion hit him hard. "Maybe we could go to different schools in the same town and share an apartment." He knew he was grasping at straws, but he couldn't help it. The thought of being separated from Kenny was nearly unbearable and he didn't know why; he just knew it was.

Kenny put his hand on Bobby's. "We've got a lot of time to worry about this later. We have to get through the SATs first." Bobby picked up the book again and began studying, but his heart just wasn't in it anymore. Putting down the book, he picked up a sketchpad.

BOBBY walked out of the testing center, his hands cramping. The SATs had been tough, but they were done. Sitting on a bench, he waited for Kenny to finish before heading home.

"How'd you do?" Kenny asked.

Bobby turned and saw him approaching. "Pretty well. I knew most of the answers without too much hesitation. You?"

Kenny took a deep breath and released it. "I'm just glad you taught me those test-taking techniques, but I think I did all right."

Bobby tossed Kenny the keys, "It's your turn to drive." They'd just gotten their licenses, and they took turns driving. Kenny caught the keys and unlocked the doors. Inside the car, they turned up the radio and sang along as Kenny drove back to the store.

Both Sean and Sam were smiling from ear to ear when they walked in. "How'd it go boys?"

"Okay."

"Good."

"That well, huh?" Sean teased, and they both rolled their eyes.

"This came for you today," Sam said, handing Kenny an envelope.

"What is it?" He looked at it and saw that it came from the Milwaukee Police Association.

"Open it and find out." Sam bounced with excitement.

Kenny ripped open the envelope and began reading the enclosed letter. "It's a scholarship letter." Kenny scowled. "I don't remember applying for anything."

"Just read the letter." Sam tried to be patient, but his own excitement colored his voice.

The three of them watched as Kenny read the letter, the scowl turning into a smile, then changing to a huge grin. "It says I qualify for a scholarship from the Police Family Benefit Fund. They'll pay half my tuition to any in-state university."

"Read further," Sam prompted.

"If I major in criminal justice or a similar law enforcement program, they'll pay all the tuition." Kenny looked around, checking all their faces like he needed to make sure it wasn't a practical joke. "Is this for real?"

"Yes. It's for real." Sam didn't elaborate on the fact that the Police Family Benefit Fund was a trust set up to help the families of fallen police officers. Sam didn't want any sadness to blight the moment.

Kenny hugged Sam and Sean and then turned to hug Bobby, but he wasn't there. Figuring that he was in the back room, Kenny raced to the stockroom to tell him. He found Bobby sitting at the table, his sketchbook open, working intently. "Did you hear?" Kenny waved the letter around before passing it to Bobby.

"Yeah, I did." He looked up from his sketch, trying to cover the sense of loss and dread that had nearly overpowered him.

Kenny sat down across from him, still smiling. "What's wrong?"

"Nothing, Kenny, there's nothing wrong." He set down his sketchbook and smiled as brightly as he could. "I'm very happy for you. This means you'll be able to go wherever you want and not have to worry." Bobby got up and walked to the other side of the table, pulling Kenny into a hug. He felt Kenny hug him back and sighed softly. He knew that Kenny thought the hug was for him, but to Bobby, it was Kenny comforting him, even if he didn't know it. He really wished he knew why he felt this way, but he didn't.

"BOBBY, you got a letter." Sean walked in the house, finding Bobby and Kenny spread out on the living room floor watching television. Bobby turned around and bounded to Sean, who handed it to him.

"It's from the school at the Art Institute of Chicago," Bobby said rather matter-of-factly and then began opening the envelope. "I've been accepted, and they've offered me a full scholarship." He sounded almost disappointed.

"I'd think you could muster a little excitement," Sean said. "That's one of the top art schools in the country. You're being offered a full scholarship, and you haven't even started your senior year. That's huge!" Sean already knew that because of an art competition Bobby had won a few years earlier, all Bobby had to do was apply and he'd have a place, thanks to Mrs. Sarah Gold, Sean's best customer. She was an extremely connected and wealthy lady who just happened to be a fan of Bobby's work. She'd brought Bobby to the attention of the director of the art institute a few years earlier.

Bobby sighed. "I know, Dad, I'm just... I don't know." He really couldn't express it, but everything seemed to bring him one step closer to a time when he and Kenny wouldn't be together any more. The thought of not being able to see him and talk to him every day scared Bobby to death. "I should be happy, and I am, but... I guess I'm a little scared."

"I know you are. I was too, when I went away to school. But you're going to meet so many interesting people, and you'll get to study with some of the most brilliant professors in the country." Sean sounded more excited than Bobby.

"You looking to get rid of me, Dad?" Bobby asked. Sean thought he was joking, but there was no smile, and Sean didn't know quite how to react.

"Sean, let me talk to him," Kenny offered, turning off the television as Sean quietly left the room. "You hurt him, you know?" Kenny looked angry. "And you're acting like an ass. He was so excited for you. By the way, do you know how important that scholarship is? How rare? How unbelievably awesome? You get to spend your entire senior year knowing which college you'll go to and that you'll get to go to one of the very best in the country. You should be happy, not questioning if Sean loves you."

Bobby knew Kenny was right and that he'd needlessly hurt Sean, but he was so scared he just couldn't help it. "It's not as though you have to leave tomorrow. You've got over a year. I'm sure you could arrange for a visit and maybe even attend a few classes to see what they're like." Leave it to Kenny to try and lift his spirits. "Now go in there and apologize to him."

Bobby grinned mischievously. "Yes, Mother," he said before dodging a slap from Kenny as he vaulted off the sofa and walked into the kitchen.

"Dad, I'm sorry," Bobby said as he walked into the kitchen and found Sean standing at the sink, doing nothing. "I shouldn't have said that."

Sean turned around. "Never doubt that I want you here or that I love you." Sean hugged him tightly. "You're growing up so fast. I thought I'd get to have you a little longer before you moved away."

"I love you too, Dad." Bobby let go and opened the refrigerator, pulling out a couple of sodas. "And I'm not gone yet," he said, smirking as Sean batted him with the dishtowel.

Bobby was already in the living room when Sean sighed. "No, you're not gone yet, but you will be soon."

Sam came in the kitchen, noticing Sean's expression. "What is it?"

"Nothing."

Sam looked down his nose. "You're feeling sad about the boys leaving, aren't you? I see that look every time they get closer to college or graduation. We've got them for at least another year, so let's make the most of it. And once they're gone, they'll be back for vacations." Sam nuzzled into Sean's neck. "And I'll get you all to myself."

"Good grief, get a room," Bobby said as he came back into the kitchen, opened the cupboard, and grabbed a bag of chips.

Sean chuckled into Sam's ear. "I'm starting to see the benefits."

"BOBBY, we're leaving." Sean's voice traveled up the stairs. Girding himself, Bobby left his bedroom and walked down the stairs, plastering a smile on his face. Sean, Sam, and Kenny were standing in the hall, excitement on their faces. "We'll be back this afternoon." The front door was open, and he could see Sam's truck, packed and ready to take Kenny off to college. "Tomorrow, we're taking you down to Chicago, so make sure you've got everything packed." Sean looked as though he was going to burst with pride and excitement.

"I will, Dad." Bobby hugged Kenny tight. "I'm going to miss you."

"I'm going to miss you too," Kenny said, holding onto Bobby tightly. "Maybe you can come to visit in Madison, and I can visit you in Chicago."

"Let's do that," Bobby said as Kenny released him. Bobby stepped back and noticed Sam and Sean walking toward the truck.

"It's going to be great, you know that." Kenny looked toward the truck. "Paint me a picture I can hang in my room." Kenny began walking toward the truck.

Bobby stood in the doorway watching as the doors closed, and the loaded truck pulled away from the curb. Once he could no longer see the truck, he closed the front door and climbed the stairs.

Bobby found himself wandering into Kenny's room. The furniture was still there, but that was pretty much it. The drawing of Kenny and Ron that always hung over the bed was gone. The closet was mostly empty, except for some lonely clothes in the back and a few things stored on the shelf. *I love you, Kenny.* The thought came unbidden to his mind, the realization hitting him hard. He loved Kenny. That's why it hurt so much to see him go. He not only loved Kenny, he was *in love* with him, and he had been for a while. "I have to get over it," he told the empty room. "I have to get over you because you don't feel the same way." If he had, then he wouldn't have left. He would have found a way for them to go to school together.

Taking a deep breath, he left the room, closing the door behind him before going back to his room to finish packing. Maybe Kenny was right—he was going to meet interesting people and learn from the most talented and the best.

His boxes sat against a wall, filled with art supplies and his sketchbooks. Sean and Sam had purchased both him and Kenny a laptop computer for graduation, and his sat in its case on top of the boxes. Opening an empty box, he began packing his new bedding and linens. Sean had taken them shopping, getting each of them everything they could possibly need and more. Next, he pulled out the suitcases and began packing his clothes.

Finally, he reached under the bed and pulled out a shoebox. Opening it, he thumbed through the pictures and mementos inside, pulling out the photograph of him and Kenny on Bedlow's Island, as well as one of the four of them taken at Mount Rushmore the previous summer.

Once his packing was complete, he wandered downstairs and through the house. In the living room, he admired the painting of Sean, Sam, and himself that Mark had done a few months after Sean had taken him in. Mark's painting of Bobby hung next to it. The other walls were filled with paintings and drawings he'd given Sean and Sam over the years, all framed with the same care as a Picasso.

The sound of the door opening pulled him out of his thoughts. He hadn't realized how much time had passed. "All packed?" Sean asked, walking into the living room.

"Yeah."

Sean sat down next to him. "You okay?"

"Yeah, just thinking." Actually he was feeling too sentimental for words, but he couldn't say that.

"What about?"

"How lucky I am." Bobby shifted to face Sean. "You took me in when I was living on the street, gave me love and more encouragement than anyone has a right to expect. You fought for me when no one else ever had." Bobby swallowed the lump in his throat. "I guess I always thought we'd have more time."

Sean chuckled. "Hey, that's my line. After all, I'm the dad here."

Bobby put his arms around Sean's neck, hugging him hard, "Thank you for…" there was just so much, it was overwhelming, "everything."

Sean squeezed him in return. "You're welcome for everything." Sean always took care of him. He wished his dad could heal the ache in his heart, but he couldn't. Only time would do that.

IT WAS Christmas, and Bobby was home, or nearly so. Making his way up the walk in darkness, he rang the bell and waited. The door opened to Sean standing in his robe. "Bobby!" Sean's face broke into a huge grin, and then Bobby was tugged into a bone-crunching hug. "I wasn't expecting you until tomorrow morning."

"I finished up today and grabbed the late train." Sean stepped aside, and Bobby picked up his suitcase, carrying it into the house. "I just couldn't wait to get home." Sean closed the door behind him, and the warmth of the house wrapped around Bobby.

"Sam's already in bed and Kenny called an hour ago. He'll be here any time now." On cue, the front door opened, and Kenny walked in carrying his own suitcase. "Merry Christmas, Kenny." Sean pulled Kenny into his arms, giving him the same kind of hug he'd given Bobby. Then Sean stepped back, smiling like the cat who'd eaten the canary. "I'm glad you're both here. Put your things upstairs and I'll get you something to eat."

They both started to say something, but Sean was already in the kitchen.

"After you, Kenny," Bobby said, watching as Kenny climbed the stairs and went directly to his room. Bobby closed the door to his room and breathed with relief. He'd been looking forward to seeing his family for weeks, but he'd missed Kenny terribly. Every time something good happened, his first impulse was to tell Kenny, and the feelings he'd hoped would fade with time had not.

After putting his things away, he opened the door, glanced at Kenny's door, and went downstairs. Reaching the bottom of the stairs, he heard happy voices. As he entered, Sam, Sean, and Kenny were all gathered around the table, Sean and Sam in their robes.

Bobby sat down, and they ate and talked. The room filled with laughter and a bit of Christmas cheer. It must have been two in the morning before they all headed upstairs to bed.

Bobby cleaned up and got ready for bed. As he was heading back from the bathroom, he found himself veering toward Kenny's closed door. Without thinking, he opened the door and quietly snuck inside. He could see Kenny's body in the bed, facing away from him. Moving quickly, he lifted the covers and climbed beneath them, putting his arms around Kenny as he snuggled close, just like he had before they'd left for college. Kenny felt so good and warm next to him, and he smelled just like he remembered.

"Bobby, we're not kids anymore," Kenny said, rolling over to face him. "We can't do this."

"I just missed you, Kenny, and we always used to sleep together." Bobby felt angry but he didn't know why.

"That was before we went to college, before we grew up."

Bobby couldn't see much in the darkness, but he heard the cold tone in Kenny's voice, and it chilled him deep down. Lifting the covers, he slipped out and walked to the door. He opened it quietly, stepped out of the room, and closed the door behind him. Walking into his room, Bobby closed the door and wiped his eyes. He had looked forward to getting back his best friend, the one he'd comforted when Kenny's dad died, the one who'd struggled through a search for identity with him, and the one he loved more than anyone else in the world.

He climbed into his own bed and turned toward the wall. "Merry Christmas," he muttered as he tried to go to sleep.

CHAPTER 7

Present day

A BANGING in the house woke Bobby from a sound sleep. It took him a minute to remember where he was. Then he figured out what the noise was. Climbing out from under the warm covers, he pulled on his robe and opened the door. Sean was carrying his suitcase down the stairs. "What time is it?" Bobby asked.

"Five-thirty." Jesus Christ, the man looked too chipper for five-thirty, but then again, he and Sam were heading to the Caribbean for a week of fun. Bobby tried to smile but yawned instead.

"Did you sleep at all?" he asked, knowing Sean tended to get all excited about things.

Sean shrugged and picked up his suitcase again, maneuvering it down the stairs. "Maybe."

"Here, let me help." Bobby picked up the case and lugged it downstairs. Sam was waiting in the front hall and took the suitcase to haul it to the curb, Chloe following his every move.

"The cab should be here in ten minutes." Sam leaned close to Sean, giving him what looked like an "I'm as excited as you are" kiss. Bobby watched through the open door as Sam bounced between excited steps.

"Hey, did a herd of elephants move in?" Kenny asked, appearing at the bottom of the stairs wearing a pair of gray sweatpants, hanging low on his hips, and apparently nothing else. Bobby did his best to avert his eyes from his broad shoulders, plates of chest muscle, and narrow waist.

Sean hugged both of them as the taxi pulled up in front of the house. "I know you'll take good care of things."

"We will, Dad. Have a great time." Bobby squeezed Sean hard. "Bring us back something." Sean chuckled as he released him and hugged Kenny, mumbling something in his ear that made him smile.

Sam raced back inside and hugged both boys. "If you have any problems, call Jerry, he'll help you." Jerry was Sam's newest partner on the force. Since Kenny's dad's death, Sam had had a number of partners. "He's a really good guy."

"We'll be fine. Just have fun." They walked out the door toward the cab, Bobby calling after them, "Don't burn your buns." Before they could respond, he closed the door and watched the taxi pull away as Kenny smacked him lightly on the shoulder. Chloe sat by the front door and whined.

"You're so bad." Then Kenny yawned. "Let's get back to bed. It's going to be a long day, and we could both use a couple more hours of sleep." Kenny tried his best to stifle another yawn but lost the battle as he turned and climbed the stairs with Bobby right behind him. Bobby turned around and saw Chloe curled up by the front door, paying no attention to them whatsoever.

Bobby watched as Kenny stepped onto the landing and walked into his room. He wanted to follow him, climb into bed with him like he used to do when they were younger. But they weren't teenagers any more, and Kenny had made his feelings perfectly clear about that. Bobby felt himself coloring slightly just thinking about it, even after all this time.

As he watched Kenny's door close, he thought of how much fun they used to have together, how much time they'd spent together, how close they'd been… once. Bobby felt hope rise again. Maybe they could be again. After all, they were going to spend the next week working together. But Bobby knew he wanted more. The feelings he thought he'd buried a long time ago began bubbling back to the surface, and he did his best to push them back, but it wasn't that easy. Resigning himself to cold reality, he stepped into his own room.

Taking off his robe, he climbed back into bed, the sheets now cold, and pulled up the blankets around his neck before falling back to sleep until the alarm sounded a few hours later.

Bobby reached to the nightstand and slapped the alarm off, debating how long he could stay in bed. Looking at the clock, he decided he couldn't and forced himself to get up. Putting his robe back on, he padded to the bathroom and got cleaned up. When he was done, he opened the door and was about to knock on Kenny's when he heard his name being spoken. Cracking the door open, he peered inside, but Kenny was still asleep. Bobby thought he was hearing things and was about to wake Kenny when he heard him mumble "Bobby" almost seductively.

"Kenny. We need to get going."

"Huh?" Kenny sat up, looking a little confused.

"You need to get cleaned up. We have to be at the store in less than an hour."

Kenny turned and looked at Bobby, a dazed expression on his face. "Yeah. I guess so." He blinked a few times and looked around the room before the expression vanished. "I'll meet you downstairs."

"I'll make coffee." Had Kenny been dreaming about him? Bobby really wanted to ask but couldn't bring himself to. What if he was wrong? He didn't want to embarrass himself, or Kenny, for that matter.

"Thank God. I haven't had decent coffee since the last time you made it for me." Kenny said as he got up, and Bobby headed to his room to get dressed.

Bobby dropped his robe and pulled on his boxers and a pair of pressed khakis before slipping on a royal blue shirt. He heard Kenny finish up in the bathroom as he finished dressing and headed downstairs.

Bobby started the coffee maker and then opened the fridge, pleasantly surprised to find that Sean had stocked it with everything he knew they liked. He should have known that his dad would make sure they were taken care of. Opening a cupboard, he got some of Chloe's food, placing it in her dish. She sniffed it and ate a little, reluctantly, it seemed to him, and then she pawed at the back door to be let out, which Bobby did right away.

"Coffee ready?" Kenny shuffled in and sat at the table, still half asleep.

"Few minutes yet. You want something to eat?" Kenny nodded and Bobby plopped some bread in the toaster, bringing butter and jam to the table. ""I was wondering how you thought we should start looking into the missing wine." The coffee finished brewing, and he brought a cup to Kenny, placing it on the table along with the toast. He sipped it, and Bobby smiled when Kenny sighed happily.

"I was thinking we should look around the back room, see if there was a place to hide anything, especially near the door. If not, maybe someone was able to get in and out. Knowing how Sean does things, I'd think it would be hard for things to disappear, and I'd be interested to talk to Jimmy."

Bobby sipped his own coffee as he sat across from Kenny. "Sam said Jimmy couldn't have taken anything. He wasn't even in the store."

"I know what Sam said, but what if the Bollinger was taken earlier, and Sean just realized it was missing later?" Kenny's eyes sparkled as he picked up his cup and began pacing the floor. "What if someone took the wine but left the case? Say they opened it from the bottom, slipped out the bottles, and left the empty case. And later, they disposed of the box. Sean would think the wine disappeared when the box did rather that when the wine was actually stolen."

Bobby had to admit, that wasn't a bad idea. "Pretty clever. Okay, so Jimmy's still on the list."

Kenny munched on his toast, nearly dripping jam on his pants. "Everyone's on the list except you and me."

"Even Katie?" Bobby found it hard to believe that Katie would take anything. She and Sean had been friends for years before opening the store. He refused to even consider it.

"Well, let me say that I doubt it's her, too, but you never know. We had a case study last term of a guy who'd worked for a small store for years and years, their best employee. Turns out he'd been stealing from them the entire time, just a little each day, every day, and no one ever noticed or looked."

"But Katie?" The thought of Katie doing anything like that was hurtful.

Kenny shook his head. "I'm not saying she did anything, just that we need to keep an open mind." He finished his coffee and toast and put the dishes in the sink.

"Okay." Bobby downed the last of his coffee. "Let's go." Bobby let the dog in and got her leash. They put on their coats and left the house, walking toward Kenny's car. He opened the door and Chloe jumped in.

Bobby was about to get in as well when Kenny threw him the keys. "Your turn to drive." Bobby couldn't help smiling as he got in and started the engine.

KENNY wandered through the bright store with Chloe right behind him, sticking to him like glue. "You get ready to open. I'll check out the stock areas and the back door, see if I can figure out anything."

"Okay." Bobby went into the office, and Kenny heard him opening the safe, and then the printer started running. Kenny walked to the small stock area behind the sales floor. There were a number of neatly stacked cases with a note on each one in Sean's familiar handwriting telling them what it was for. Kenny shook his head and kept wandering, looking for something, anything, that shouldn't be there. The back door fire exit was solid and had a panic alarm. He pushed it and it went off, Chloe raised her head and howled but made no move to go outside. Then he realized he didn't have the key to stop it.

"Need these?"

Bobby threw him the keys. Kenny checked outside, shut the door, and turned off the alarm before throwing the keys back.

"Anything?" Bobby asked.

"Not yet." Kenny went back to his examinations. There were a few small windows, but they'd been filled in with glass block. There was only the door to the store, the alarmed back door, and the door to the office. Kenny heard Bobby finishing up in the office and the safe closing before he heard Bobby walking into the store and then the sound of the register being opened. Kenny wandered out behind him, standing near the counter, while Chloe settled into what was obviously her cushion. "Near as I can figure, there are two ways the wine disappeared. One is through the front door, and the other is out with the trash. I can't see a way for someone to get in or out otherwise."

"So what you're saying is that someone walked though the store and carried out a case of wine without being noticed, or somehow the bottles got out the back door, either in the trash or by someone with a key." Bobby finished opening the register. "I checked the inventory. It shows fifteen bottles of Bollinger, but I could only locate three. So a case does indeed appear to be missing."

"Damn, I was hoping it was just a mistake."

"We have to open the store," Bobby said, unlocking the front door and putting out the signboard. He looked up and down the deserted street. "Looks like we're in for a slow morning." No sooner were the words out of Bobby's mouth than a car pulled up in front and a group of ladies got out and wandered into the store, beginning the sales day.

Kenny spent much of the morning and afternoon helping customers. When he wasn't doing that, he washed the tasting glasses. A few times, he took Chloe for a walk, but on the whole, he didn't leave the store for very long. At dinnertime, he walked to the deli and got sandwiches for himself and Bobby, and they ate behind the counter between customers. As they were finishing up, Jimmy came in, smiling as he approached the counter. "Hey, Bobby, Kenny. Did Sean and Sam get off okay?" Chloe perked up and rolled over so he could rub her tummy.

"They should be in the land of sun and sand by now." Bobby replied.

Jimmy looked outside into the cold March darkness and sighed. "I'll start getting things cleaned up."

"Thanks." Bobby smiled and watched as Jimmy disappeared in back, only to return with a broom and dust mop and start to work, Chloe following him the entire time.

Kenny looked at Bobby who looked back at him and shrugged. As soon as Jimmy finished sweeping and went in the back, Kenny asked, "What do we do?"

"Give him an opportunity and see if he takes it. I'll open the back door so he can take out the trash. As soon as I do, you call me, so I have to step away. After closing, we'll wait and see if anyone shows up to check."

The plan went like clockwork, sort of. Kenny unlocked the door, and Bobby called him as soon as the door was open. He went to see what Bobby wanted and returned to find Jimmy standing near the door.

"You need to lock it," he said. Kenny did and Jimmy went back to work, smiling as he petted Chloe before filling her bowl with food. This time Kenny noticed that Chloe emptied the dish. The dog obviously adored Jimmy.

At closing, Bobby closed out the register and locked the door behind Jimmy. Kenny watched as the teenager waved and got into a car with what looked like his mother behind the wheel. "Somehow, I don't think our plan was successful."

"How come?" Bobby asked as he finished working on the register and removed the cash drawer, carrying it back to the office.

Kenny began laughing. "Because I think his mother just picked him up," he replied as he followed Bobby into the office.

"Well, what do we do now?"

"Check the trash to make sure. And we could watch the alley to see if we see anything. If stuff's disappearing, it's probably through the back door." While staking out the alley probably wasn't the most fun thing they could do, it was an excuse to spend time alone with Bobby.

"I'm game if you're game."

After locking everything up, Bobby got Chloe, and they turned out the lights and left through the front door, walking to Kenny's car and climbing in. "I'll drive around the block and park in the lot at the end of the alley. We should be able to see fairly well." Kenny started the car and pulled out, following his plan and parking at the end of the alley. "Stay here with Chloe and I'll check the Dumpster."

"Okay."

Kenny got out of the car and walked cautiously toward the Dumpster, lifting the lid and pulling out the trash bag from the store. It seemed heavy. Putting the bag on the ground, he opened it to find wine bottles, all empty. "Shit, what a waste of time." Reclosing the bag, he put it back in the Dumpster and walked toward the car.

"Anything?"

Kenny settled in the driver's seat. "Just the empties from tasting."

"What now?" Bobby asked. The cold was beginning to seep into the car, and Kenny felt Bobby scoot closer. This time, he didn't shy away. Extending his arm, he rubbed Bobby's shoulder, feeling his weight against his side. This was nice, really nice.

Kenny shrugged against Bobby's shoulder. "Let's wait and see if something happens."

"If someone was getting in the store through the back, they'd take a lot more than a case or two of wine. They'd clean out the store."

Kenny was about to agree and start the car when he saw movement in the alley. "Look." He pointed to what looked like a figure walking close to the wall, stopping outside the door to the store and staying there. Chloe began growling. "Let's go." Kenny opened his door and Chloe jumped out over him, barking as she ran down the alley, her leash trailing after her. "Shit!" Kenny took off after her with Bobby right behind him. Chloe stopped at the door, growling, but staying back.

"Please don't let the dog hurt me." Kenny grabbed Chloe's leash as he and Bobby stared into the eyes of what looked like a scared kid, one who couldn't have been more than ten years old. "Please don't hurt me," he pleaded and then began to cry, holding his hands in front of his face.

CHAPTER 8

WITH those big eyes staring up at him, so helpless and scared, Bobby remembered what that felt like. "No one's going to hurt you." This was the last thing he expected to find. "I promise." The crying tapered off, but those eyes were still so full of tears. "What's your name?"

"Tommy." The high voice was brimming with fear as the boy looked around, eyes darting to Kenny, Chloe, and then back to Bobby.

"Okay, Tommy. I'm Bobby, and that's Kenny." Bobby saw Tommy's fear rise as Kenny got closer, so he motioned for Kenny to back away. "Did you run away?" The response was a slow nod. "Why?"

"'Cause Mommy and Daddy don't love me anymore." Tears started in earnest again, and Bobby couldn't help himself. He reached out and hugged the youngster to him, letting him cry on his shoulder.

"Bobby." He looked over Tommy's shoulder and up at Kenny. "We should get out of this alley," Kenny continued.

Bobby nodded and returned his attention to Tommy. "Will you come with us to the car?"

He shook his head vigorously. "Mommy says I'm not supposed to get in the car with strangers." Tommy wiped his nose on his sleeve.

"Why do you think your mommy and daddy don't love you?"

Bobby could tell Tommy was about two seconds from crying again. "They fight all the time, yelling and screaming," he said.

Bobby heard footsteps retreating and realized Kenny was putting Chloe back in the car. A few minutes later he returned. "I called Jerry and he's on his way."

Bobby breathed a sigh of relief. Jerry would know exactly what to do. "What do they yell about?"

Tommy shrugged, "They just yell, and I hide under my bed. Sometimes they yell at me too. I think they're gonna get a divorce."

"When did you leave?"

"After dinner. Mom made macaroni and cheese."

Thank God he'd only been on the streets a few hours. Bobby breathed a huge sigh of relief. He said a silent prayer of thanks that he and Kenny had found him before someone else had, someone more dangerous. "Where do you live?"

"Whitefish Bay." Bobby's questions seemed to be having a calming effect on Tommy.

That was on the other side of town. "How'd you get here?"

"I took the bus, but I ran out of money and I had to get off." Bobby wanted to scream. Some bus driver dropped a kid off after dark and all alone. Bobby made a note to be sure to tell that to Jerry when he arrived.

Bobby kept Tommy talking until he saw headlights skim down the alley and a car park next to Kenny's. "Who's that?" The fear rose in Tommy's voice.

"That's a friend of ours. His name's Jerry. He's a nice policeman, and he's going to help you." Jerry approached and knelt down in front of Tommy, trying not to alarm him. "Jerry, this is Tommy."

"Hi, Tommy. I think we need to take you home. Your mom's been very worried about you."

"She has?" Tommy lifted his head, looking at Jerry very suspiciously. "How do you know?"

"Because she called and told us. She's been scared and worried since she realized you were gone." Jerry stood up and put out his hand. "You can ride with me in the police car." Tommy didn't take Jerry's hand. Instead, he latched onto Bobby and refused to let go. Jerry smiled and lowered his hand. "Bobby will ride along with you." Jerry led the way to the police car, Bobby and Tommy getting into the back seat.

"I'll follow you so I can bring Bobby home," Kenny said as he opened the door to his car. Jerry waved and got inside, starting the engine.

Bobby expected Tommy to ask if Jerry could turn on the siren, but he didn't. In fact, he said nothing at all, did nothing at all except look out the window. "It's going to be okay."

Tommy's face turned to Bobby's, his big eyes looking so sad. "What if she doesn't want me?"

Bobby could almost feel his heart breaking. Suddenly he was Tommy, remembering what it was like to be on the streets alone, knowing that no one wanted him, no one loved him. He shivered when he remembered the nights he'd spent out in the cold, huddled in a doorway. Bobby got his thoughts under control—this wasn't helping Tommy.

"Your mom loves you. Sometimes moms and dads fight, but it's not your fault, and it doesn't mean they don't love you."

The car pulled onto a tree-lined street with decorative street lights and beautiful stone houses. "That's my house," Tommy said, his voice full of only nerves and fear.

The car stopped, and Jerry got out, opening the car door as Kenny pulled up behind them. As soon as Tommy got out, the front door of the house opened and a woman ran down the walk, scooping Tommy into her arms, crying as she cradled her son.

"You scared me so much," she said. Bobby heard Tommy crying too. "I love you, Tommy, love you so much." She continued crying as she stood up, continuing to hold Tommy close. "Thank you for finding him," she said, as a man, presumably Tommy's father, joined Tommy's mom on the sidewalk. Bobby noticed that he had tears in his eyes as well.

"I didn't." Jerry indicated Bobby. "Bobby and Kenny found him in an alley off Broadway."

"Thank you both," she said, still holding her son.

"Yes, thank you. I can't tell you how relieved we are that he's home safe." Tommy's dad stepped forward, shaking both their hands and thanking them, the worry and fear easing from his expression.

"Can I get you anything, a cup of coffee?"

Jerry responded for them all. "No, thank you, ma'am. I just a have a few questions and then we have to get going." Jerry talked to Tommy's parents, taking notes as he went along.

Bobby watched as the three of them proceeded up the walk. Then he saw Tommy rush back down. "Thank you, Bobby," the boy said as Bobby leaned down and Tommy threw his arms around his neck, hugging him hard. "I gotta go." Bobby watched Tommy run toward the house, the front door closing behind him.

Bobby was surprised by Jerry's hand on his shoulder. "That was a really good thing you did, and I'm glad you guys called," he said. "Tomorrow, I'll have to write up a report, and Tommy's parents will get a follow-up visit from child services, but it looks like Tommy's going to be fine." Jerry got in his car and drove off, and Bobby got in Kenny's car, sitting silently as Kenny drove them home.

"Are you okay? You've been too quiet."

Bobby felt as though he'd been transported back through time, and not in a good way. "I've been thinking about the months I spent living on the streets before Dad took me in." Kenny pulled up in front of the house and turned off the engine, but Bobby made no move to get out of the car. "I spent months living off what I could beg or steal. In the summer, it wasn't so bad, but the winter nights were tough."

"You've never told me about it."

"I know. The only one I've ever told is Dad, and once I did, I tried to put it behind me. But seeing Tommy's scared face brought back all the memories: sleeping in doorways, living in a plywood shelter, the winter cold, and oppressive summer heat. Most of which I never wanted to remember."

"Let's go inside," Kenny said. Bobby nodded and followed him and Chloe into the house, going right upstairs to his room.

KENNY watched as Bobby slowly climbed the stairs. He wanted to reach out and hold him, make him feel better, but he didn't know if Bobby would let him. With all the time and distance between them, he wasn't Bobby's comforter any longer. They weren't kids any more. Wandering into the kitchen, he got a drink and then closed up the house before going upstairs.

Bobby's door was closed, but Kenny walked up to it and listened but heard nothing. Carefully, he walked to his own door before stopping. *Grow a pair.* Kenny went back to Bobby's door and knocked softly before opening it. The room was dark, but in the light from the hall, he could see Bobby lying on the bed, still in his clothes. "Bobby?"

"Yeah?"

Was that a sniffle? Kenny walked in the room and sat on the edge of the bed. "Are you crying?" He didn't get an answer, so he assumed a yes. "Why?"

"I don't know." Bobby rolled away, and even in the dim light, Kenny could see Bobby's shoulders raising and lowering.

Suddenly they were kids again and the intervening years weren't so important. "Shhh, it's okay." Kenny rubbed his hand over Bobby's back, trying to soothe as best he could. He wasn't very good at this sort of thing. It was Bobby who usually soothed him, who comforted him and made things better.

"I know. I'm just being stupid." Bobby sat up and wiped his eyes.

"No, you're not. You said Tommy brought back a lot of memories, and I bet a lot of feelings you haven't thought about or dealt with. It's okay to be sad and it's okay to cry."

"Tommy's so lucky. He has two parents who love him. My mom gave me up because she wanted her drugs more than she wanted me. And my father...." Kenny listened as Bobby's voice trailed off. He almost asked about Bobby's biological dad but let it drop. "No one loved me until I met Sean." Bobby actually smiled. "He got me warm and bought me lunch. I thought that was it and walked away, but you know Dad." He did. Kenny knew Sean would never leave someone in need if he could do something about it. "He took me back to the store, gave me some work to do, and then took me home." The tears started again. "That was the best day of my life, up until then."

"What was the best day of your life since then?" If Bobby was going to wander down memory lane, Kenny was going to help him. Maybe Bobby would feel better.

"The day Dad adopted me. Followed by the day I met my best friend." Kenny didn't know how to reply. He thought Bobby was going to say more, but he didn't.

"I remember that day," Kenny said. "You walked into history class and sat next to me. You didn't say much, but I talked enough for both of us." He saw Bobby nod and smile. "We kept talking for most of the rest of the term, but I knew you were my best friend when you told me you were gay. And then you helped me get through it." Kenny felt sort of wistful. "You were the best friend I ever had."

"Were?" He could hear the hurt in Bobby's voice.

"You are my best friend. The best I ever had." Kenny wanted to keep Bobby talking and thought a change of topic would be good. "You told me you have a senior project. Have you decided on anything?"

"No. I thought about painting Dad, but I've done that already, and they're going to want something important and meaningful. I just wish I could think of something. I've been blocked for a while." Bobby reclined against the headboard, looking much more relaxed and definitely less upset. "I just wish I could come up with a good idea."

"You will." Kenny slipped off his shoes and reclined on the bed next to Bobby. Once he'd done it, he realized how natural it felt and how automatically he'd done it. "I have faith in you."

"Everyone tells me I can't rush it and that the idea will come to me. I just need to be patient." Bobby chuckled softly and Kenny joined in. He knew how impatient Bobby could be sometimes.

"They're probably right, and it'll come to you when you least expect it. My best ideas always come to me when I'm thinking about something else."

Bobby rolled onto his side, his arm resting across Kenny's chest, a small sigh escaping his lips. "I've really missed this—you know, being close to you like this." Kenny could hear the angst and longing in Bobby's voice, and he felt a knot in his stomach melt away. He hadn't messed their friendship up. Maybe they could be as close as they once were.

"I missed it too." Kenny put an arm under Bobby's neck, bringing them closer. "After Dad died, you were the one who looked after me and got me through. I'll never forget the way you held me that night. After all I'd been through, you made me feel safe." Bobby moved closer, putting his head on Kenny's shoulder. Kenny turned and saw Bobby's deep blue eyes staring back at him, those lips so close to his. He wanted to taste them, find out how they'd feel against his. He wanted to satisfy a curiosity he'd had for a long time about how it would feel to kiss Bobby. He saw Bobby's tongue dart across those lips, wetting them, he even thought he saw Bobby's head move closer.

Then the phone rang and they both jumped. "One guess," Kenny said, getting off the bed and answering the phone in Sean and Sam's room.

"Hi, Kenny."

"Hi, Sean. You and Sam having a good time?"

"Yeah, we are." Kenny could hear music and people in the background. "We're at a buffet and I actually got a signal, so I thought I'd call. I tried earlier but no one was home."

Kenny explained about Tommy and helping to get him back to his parents. He left out the fact that they were staking out the alley when they found him. "We got home less than an hour ago."

"Is everything okay at the store?"

"Everything's fine. Business was good." Kenny could hear a crackling on the line. "I'm about to lose you. Have fun." Sean said something, but Kenny didn't catch it as the line faded to nothing. Hanging up the phone, he wandered back into Bobby's room. It didn't look as though Bobby had moved at all. In fact, it looked like Bobby was waiting for him to come back.

"That was Sean. They're having fun." Bobby smiled and nodded gently. "We should get to sleep. We've got another long day ahead of us." Kenny left the room and went to his own, getting ready for bed. Pulling back the covers, he was about to get in bed when he changed his mind. What's the worst that could happen? *Bobby could tell me no.* It was time he made up for that Christmas those years ago, and maybe, just maybe, the thaw he'd felt starting could become another spring.

The house was dark, but he didn't need light to know where he was going. Carefully, he opened the door. "Bobby."

"Hmmm." He saw those eyes pierce the darkness, big and bright, maybe a little hopeful? That glimmer of hope spurred him on.

Kenny slipped into the room and lifted the covers, sliding in next to Bobby. "You still wear pajamas?" Kenny asked, and Bobby chuckled sleepily.

"In the winter. I get cold, okay?" Kenny nodded against Bobby's shoulder. He smelled so good and felt so warm against him. Kenny slipped his hand across Bobby's stomach and pulled him closer, just like when Bobby had comforted him all those years ago. He still wasn't sure if he'd be welcome, but he got his answer when Bobby's hand laced with his and held on. Kenny smiled and thanked the powers that be for the return of his best friend. If Bobby didn't want anything more, he could live with it, but being this close made him want Bobby sleeping with him all the time. He just wished Bobby felt the same way.

Bobby scooted closer, and Kenny felt his own body react to the closeness. He almost moved away but didn't. When Bobby didn't say anything, he relaxed and let himself fall asleep.

Chapter 9

BOBBY woke to warmth pressed against his back and arms around him. It felt really nice, and he was afraid to move. He knew that Kenny was just comforting him, and he colored with embarrassment when he remembered his reaction the night before. But this felt so nice, and he wished it could happen every night. What he wouldn't give to be able to tell Kenny how he felt and to have his feelings returned.

They were just getting close again after all those years of distance, and he didn't want to do anything to jeopardize things. He wouldn't risk Kenny's friendship. That was too precious. So he lay there in the darkness, afraid to close his eyes, listening to Kenny's breathing and feeling the rise and fall of his chest as wishes and wonderings floated through his mind.

He must have dozed off, because when he opened his eyes again, the room was flooded with light and he was alone in the bed. He knew he should have expected it, but his stomach knotted with disappointment anyway. Damn it—when was he going to learn that Kenny was his friend and there could be nothing more between them. Kenny just wasn't interested. His actions had told him that enough times. But Bobby just couldn't get his heart to listen, no matter how hard he tried. With a sigh, he forced away his maudlin thoughts before climbing out of bed and heading to the bathroom.

As he approached the door, he heard the shower and something else. The door, which never closed all the way without a hard push, was slightly ajar. Bobby couldn't see inside, and he really didn't look. He didn't need too. The soft moans and throaty mumbles told him exactly what Kenny was doing. Bobby couldn't help it—he closed his eyes and imagined how Kenny looked right now, fingers wrapped around himself, stroking, maybe the other hand pinching one of the nipples that Bobby longed to pluck. Or maybe his other hand was slick, a finger sliding into himself. Bobby shuddered at the vision that flashed through his mind and had to stop his hand from sliding into his pajama bottoms.

A more forceful moan floated out of bathroom carried on the sound of the water. The deep throaty tone's signal was unmistakable. Bobby closed his eyes again, letting his imagination take over. He could see Kenny standing under the water, fingers sliding, eyes closed, an expression of sweet, blissful agony on his face as it registered his impending, forceful climax. The pleasurable pressure building, his body reacting, the climax getting closer and closer, reaching the peak until—

"Bobby."

His eyes flew open, and he backed away from the door. Had he really heard that? He backed away farther. It must have been his imagination. He heard the sound of the water stop and then the shower door open and close. He started walking backward; he needed to make it to his room. He'd die of embarrassment if Kenny found him. He heard Chloe bounding up the stairs, and she nearly collided with him as she raced into his room. Making it to the door, he slowly closed it and waited on the other side, listening for Kenny and replaying things in his mind. He still wasn't sure if he'd actually heard Kenny calling his name. And the more he thought about it, though he hoped it was true, he figured it was just his imagination. He wasn't lucky enough for it to be otherwise.

Hearing footsteps, he opened his door as Kenny was entering his own room, Chloe rushing out to greet him. "You might want to give it a few minutes," he said. "There may not be much hot water left." Kenny looked apologetic and Bobby bit back the sarcastic "thanks" that nearly came out. "I'm sorry," Kenny added, and he hurried into his room with Chloe and closed the door. Bobby couldn't stop the smile when he saw the color that rose in Kenny's cheeks. Stepping into the bathroom, he got cleaned up before opening the shower and turning on the water.

The water was still hot as he washed himself, running soapy hands over his skin. It took mere seconds for the scene he'd just imagined to flash in his mind. His slick hands stroked and he bit his lip to keep any sound from escaping. He was so worked up, it didn't take but a few seconds before his knees quivered, and his hands shook as he reached a blinding climax, hearing Kenny's voice moan his name.

The water began to chill quickly, so he finished up and turned it off. Drying himself, he fastened the towel around his waist and padded back to the bedroom to dress.

Dressed for the day, Bobby went downstairs, the scent of breakfast drawing him like a moth to flame. "Is that bacon?" he asked.

"I figured it was the fastest way to get you moving."

Bobby picked up a piece and took a bite. "Food of the gods." Chloe sat nearby, watching every bite he took.

"At least the god of cholesterol," Kenny said. Bobby tried to snag another piece, but Kenny stopped him. "Hey, that's for both of us, you know." He moved the plate to the other side of the stove. "Set the table, would you?"

Bobby munched on the bacon as he got the plates and silverware before pouring glasses of orange juice and then feeding Chloe. The toaster popped, and Kenny brought the food to the table, sitting in the chair opposite Bobby. They ate in silence. Bobby searched for something to say but couldn't think of anything, so he lowered his eyes and ate quietly.

"Have you given any more thought to what happened to the case of Bollinger?" Kenny asked between bites.

Bobby took another piece of bacon. "I'm starting to think that Dad's mistaken. It doesn't look like it could get out the front of the store, and the back door seems secure. So unless Katie or Laura took it, which is highly unlikely, it's almost got to be some sort of mistake." He didn't really believe it, but it was the best explanation he had.

Kenny's expression showed the same skepticism that Bobby felt. "It could be, but you know Laura, she double and triple checks every entry she makes. And Sean knows his stock so well. I swear he wouldn't need to even look at the inventory. He can probably recite it from memory. No, I think there's something going on. We just aren't looking at this the right way."

Bobby huffed softly as he ate. "What other way is there?"

"I'm not sure yet. But we need to keep our eyes and ears open. The Bollinger's long gone, but we can make damn sure nothing else sprouts legs." Kenny munched on a piece of toast. "But if it does...." Kenny didn't finish his thought. He didn't need to. The steely look in his eyes told Bobby everything he needed to know and turned him on at the same time. That hard-as-nails look settled right in Bobby's groin. He knew he didn't want to be on the receiving end of that look... unless it was in bed.

"God, you've gotten stubborn," Bobby said, winking as he swallowed and got up to put his dishes in the dishwasher.

"No more than you." Kenny pushed back his chair. "You remember when I first came to live here after my dad died? I wanted to stay in my room all the time, and you refused to let me. Every time I turned around, you were pulling me somewhere, and the more I said no, the more you forced me to get out. God, you were so stubborn."

"I'm only stubborn when I'm right." Bobby grinned. "And since I'm never wrong—" Bobby jumped away with a laugh as Kenny snapped a dishcloth at him, and they both began laughing while Chloe raced around the kitchen, barking happily, ready to play.

Putting down the cloth, Kenny quickly cleaned up the counter before starting the dishwasher. "We need to get going."

"I know." Bobby let the smile fade from his face. "I wanted to thank you for last night. Tommy really got to me. I just kept thinking of all the things that could happen to him and that kept bringing me to what could have happened to me."

Kenny pulled him into a hug. "I know," he said. "But those things didn't happen to him, mainly because of you. You helped him. You knew how to talk to him, and you got him to open up. I couldn't have done that."

"Sure you could."

Kenny shook his head. "No, I couldn't. You got him to open up because you understood what he was feeling. You understood his fear, because you've felt that same fear. I really haven't, not to that degree anyway."

"Well, thank you for being there for me," Bobby said as Kenny's hand stroked his cheek. The touch was so sweet and intimate that he wasn't quite sure how to react. Looking into Kenny's eyes, he saw the soft look and held still, hoping Kenny wouldn't stop.

But Kenny's hand slipped away. "We need to go." Bobby nodded and got his coat. He attached Chloe's leash to her collar, locked the house behind him, and followed Kenny to the car.

KENNY drove and Bobby rode. They were both quiet, which was frustrating for Kenny. He could have kicked himself for getting out of bed and not waiting for Bobby to wake up, but it was the right thing to do. Bobby had needed him last night, and he'd been there for him. Their friendship was too important, and if he'd stayed in bed, he wasn't sure he could have kept his hands off him. He'd been in a perpetual state of arousal since he woke up, and even taking care of himself in the shower hadn't done a damn thing except fuel his vivid imagination. He just hoped the noise of the shower had covered his groans.

When they arrived at the store, Kenny was surprised to see the lights already on. Parking, they got out and unlocked the door. "Who's here?"

"Hey, Kenny," Laura called out from the office. "Is Bobby with you?" A second later, they saw her striding toward the front of the store. "I thought I'd get a jump on the books." She hugged both of them. "So, you're manning the store while they're off sunning themselves."

"Yup." Bobby grinned. "We're slaving away here while they're roasting their rumps in the Caribbean." He unclipped Chloe's leash and slipped off his coat.

Laura snorted in a very unladylike manner. "Can you see Sean lying out naked to get a tan?" She snorted again. "After five minutes in the sun, that lily-white rear of his would be lobster red. What a way to ruin a vacation—sunburned butt."

Kenny watched as she and Bobby wandered back toward the office, still laughing, while he did another survey of the stockroom, finding nothing amiss. Returning to the sales floor, he found Bobby getting the register ready to open. "Find anything?" Bobby closed the cash drawer as the register spit out the opening register receipts.

"Nothing that wasn't there yesterday," Kenny said as he began pulling out the bottles for tasting. "We're almost sold out of the pinot. What did Sean plan as the replacement?" Kenny got the three other wines ready.

"I'll go get it." Bobby stepped around the counter and walked to the office. Kenny finished getting things ready, moving the last of the pinot to the stock and making a place in the tasting display for the replacement. "Kenny, could you look at this?"

Something in Bobby's voice made him hurry. "What is it?"

Bobby pointed. "Look. Dad's left a list of wines for tasting. He wanted us to replace the pinot with this Coppola Cabernet." Bobby showed him the note. "There are supposed to be five cases, and there were yesterday, but there's only four now." Bobby showed him the cases and Kenny could see them numbered two of five, three of five, etc. "Where's case one of five?"

Kenny looked toward the office. "Check the stock room, I'll be right back." Kenny unlocked the back door and went into the alley, the cold morning air raising goose bumps on his skin. Lifting the lid of the Dumpster, he peered inside, fighting his gag reflex. But all he saw were the bags from the night before and a few boxes. Closing the lid, he continued down the alley and around the side until he found Laura's small SUV. Peeking in the windows, he could see the spotless interior. In the back, he saw what looked like a wine case. Moving to the back window her peered inside. It was indeed a wine box, filled with notebooks. "Damn it!!!" He was frustrated and relieved at the same time. He didn't want it to be any of Sean's employees. Both Laura and Katie had been friends since he came to live with Sean and Sam. The two women had helped see him through the grief of losing his father. He desperately didn't want either of them to be stealing from the store.

He was shivering as he made his way back to the stock room door and let himself inside, closing and locking the door. "Find anything?" Bobby asked.

Kenny jumped and turned around. "No." He kept his voice down, his teeth still chattering.

Bobby began rubbing Kenny's arms. "You're so cold," he said, continuing to rub and stroke Kenny. He rubbed up and down his arms and then made big circles on his back, hands slipping beneath his shirt. Kenny had to clench his teeth to keep from making happy sounds. Bobby's smooth hands on his skin felt so good. "Better?"

"Yeah, thank you." Bobby's hands slipped away and Kenny wanted to ask him to continue but stopped himself as he started to wonder what those hands would feel like on the rest of his body. He needed to distract himself from his thoughts. "Is there a camera back here?"

"I don't think so. Dad just had them installed in the sales floor. Why?"

He put his hand to his lips. "Let's get this wine display built before we open." Bobby signaled that he understood Kenny's message. They hauled the wine out front and began building the display. "Once Laura leaves, I'm going to scan the tapes to check for anything. I'm not hopeful, but you never know." Kenny stacked the wine on the floor while Bobby cut the top box for display purposes. "I checked the trash and her car, but found nothing." Kenny could feel his own energy and tension rising. "I don't like this. Either it's one of Sean's employees, or someone is getting in here somehow. When was it you last saw all five cases?" Kenny finished putting the last case on the stack.

"Just before we closed. They were right near the stockroom door."

"After the trash was taken out?"

"Yes." He put the display case on top and went behind the counter to make up the price sign.

"This is fucking weird."

"I know." Bobby finished the sign and placed it on the display. "It's almost time to open." Bobby turned the knob on the front door and moved the sandwich board onto the sidewalk while Kenny did some cleaning and wondered what in the hell was going on and what he was missing.

Laura left an hour later with hugs and a wave. Kenny was finally able to get into the office. He reviewed the tapes from all the cameras, but they showed nothing except an empty store during the night and Laura opening the front door that morning, locking it behind her, the lights coming on, and her walking through the store to the office. "Anything?"

"No. Nothing at all."

"Okay. Leave it for now. We're starting to get busy." Bobby left and went back to the sales floor. Kenny reset the monitors to the current images and followed Bobby. As he stepped onto the floor, he saw a woman enter the store. She saw Bobby and walked right up to him. She looked familiar, so Kenny walked to the counter. "Kenny, this is Tommy's mom, Bernice." That's why she was familiar.

"I just wanted to stop in and thank both of you for helping my son." Chloe got up from her bed in the corner, walking over and nearly sitting on Bobby's shoes. She obviously missed her daddy. "I don't know what would have happened if you hadn't found him." Kenny saw a tear run down her cheek.

"How'd you find us?" Kenny inquired, trying to keep his voice pleasant.

She pulled a tissue out of her purse. "Tommy told me where he was, and I started going into every store until I found you." She dabbed her eyes. "I just had to thank you."

Both Kenny and Bobby smiled. "We're just glad we could help and that he's okay," Kenny said in his best policeman-in-training voice.

"He seems like a very nice kid. We're both glad he was only scared and not hurt." Bobby interjected as Chloe began to wind her way through the woman's legs.

"Is this the dog Tommy told me about?"

Bobby began laughing as he took her collar and pulled her back. "Yeah, she bounded out of the car before we could stop her. She barked a lot, but she'd never hurt anyone. I think she scared Tommy, though."

She sighed, "I don't know why he ran away. He won't tell us." She wiped her eyes again with the tissue.

Bobby looked at Kenny and then back at Bernice, saying nothing. Kenny was about to say something, and he shook his head slightly. "Once Tommy's calmed down and no longer scared, ask him again. He needs to tell you and you need to listen."

"Did he say anything last night?"

Bobby looked her directly in the face. "He may have, but you need to hear it from him and he needs to tell you." There was a line forming at the register, and Bobby excused himself and began ringing up customers.

"I shouldn't take up so much of your time."

Kenny walked her to the door. "If after a few days he still refuses to tell you, come back and see us." She nodded her thanks and left the store. Kenny watched her leave and started helping other customers.

Chapter 10

BOBBY was feeling that itch and it was becoming hard to concentrate. They'd had a steady stream of customers, but when things had slowed down, they retreated to the office where Bobby's pencil was now skimming over the surface of his sketchpad.

"Bobby, we're getting busy again."

He didn't turn his head. "Okay, I'm on my way." But he didn't hear Kenny's footsteps as he walked out of the office. His mind immediately slipped back to his drawing.

"Bobby!"

"Sorry!" He put down the pad and hightailed it to the sales floor and got to work, but his mind remained back in the office with his sketchpad. Business began to slow again, and Bobby retrieved his pad, sitting on a stool behind the counter.

"Sometimes your talent just blows me away." Bobby turned around and saw Kenny peering over his shoulder. "That's a great drawing of Tommy." Bobby looked up and saw Jimmy sweeping the floors. He's been so engrossed in what he was doing, he hadn't realized Jimmy had come in or how late it was getting.

"I'm sorry. When I'm working I lose track of everything around me."

Kenny chuckled. "I noticed. The building could have burned down, and you'd still be sitting on your stool as the roof caved in."

Bobby closed the pad and put it on the table behind the counter. "I've been thinking," Kenny whispered. "Dad never put cameras in the stock areas of the store. I'm going to try to move one back there after we close. Who knows, maybe we'll get lucky."

Bobby began cleaning up the tasting area. "Won't Laura or Katie notice the change when they're in the office?"

"I'll set that camera to record but not show on the monitors. We'll be able to check it if something else goes missing."

"Sounds like a good idea, but we'll have to put the camera back before Dad gets home." Bobby finished his cleaning and poured each of them a taste of the cabernet. He handed a glass to Kenny and took a sip. "This is really nice."

Kenny nodded as he finished his taste and washed both their glasses. "We need to close soon, and I want to start on the camera modifications."

"What do you want me to do?"

Kenny picked up the sketchbook and handed it to Bobby. "I think something's calling you." Bobby looked up and found himself eye to eye with Kenny. They were so close he could feel Kenny's breath on his lips. Without thinking Bobby tilted his head and parted his lips. He could tell by the look on Kenny's face that he wanted this too, the desire was there, plain for anyone to see.

"I'm ready to take out the trash." Kenny pulled away, and they both looked toward Jimmy as he approached the counter. "Am I interrupting something?" They must have looked guilty because Bobby saw Jimmy flush with embarrassment.

Kenny recovered his composure first. "No, we were discussing some plans for a display Sean wanted us to put together." Bobby watched as Kenny and Jimmy walked through the store to the stockroom, and Bobby turned his attention to something nuzzling against his leg.

"Hey, girl." He reached down to stroke Chloe's head. "You're such a good dog, aren't you?" She leaned against him as he stroked her. "You miss your daddy, don't you?" She looked up at him, her boxer face so expressive. "Yeah, you do, I can tell, but you've got a few more days with us." He continued the rubbing. "After we close, I'll take you for a good walk. How's that?"

The front door opened, and a few customers entered. Chloe wandered over to investigate, where she got strokes and scratches behind the ears before going back to settle on her cushion. The customers wandered around and Bobby poured them a few tastes. Making their purchases, they left the store, and Bobby locked up after them and began the closing process.

Jimmy came out of the back, walking toward the counter. "Is there anything else?"

"I don't think so." Bobby met him at the door and let him out. "We'll see you Tuesday." Jimmy got into his mother's car and they drove away, both of them waving. Bobby spent the next little while closing up everything before turning off the lights on the sales floor. In the back, he found Kenny already on a ladder, his head above the ceiling. "Is it going to work?"

"Yes, but it'll take awhile." He didn't stop what he was doing, so his voice was garbled, but Bobby got the gist of it. "I think I'm going to need to get some parts tomorrow."

"Call if you need help." Bobby thought he heard Kenny scoff as he walked into the office with Chloe right behind him. Settling on the futon, he opened his sketchbook and began to draw. Chloe jumped up and curled next to him. The images in his mind became more vivid and realistic, their lines flowing down his arm to his fingers and then onto the paper. The world narrowed to his vision, the pencil, and paper—nothing else existed right then. Bobby felt blissful and untouchable as he worked.

"Bobby. Bobby." He heard the voice on the edge of his consciousness and it gradually grew. He became aware of Chloe jumping down and then someone sitting next to him, touching his arm. "Bobby." The visions faded and he looked into Kenny's eyes.

"Sorry."

"Don't be. You were working so hard, I hated to disturb you, but it's getting late." Kenny looked at the sketchbook. "Does this mean that you're getting ideas again?"

"Maybe. I don't know, but I'm hoping this signals that the creative block I've had is fading." He patted the seat and Chloe jumped back on the futon. "How about you? Have you made any headway deciding what you want to do?"

Kenny shook his head. "No," he sighed heavily. "I think I chose this path because of my dad, but I don't know if it's right for me. I wish I had your talent, something that I could do better than anyone else. I mean, you know what you want to do and what you love."

"So do you. You want to help people, and you're good at it. I can see you being the best police officer ever. You have what most officers don't. You had your dad and Sam as role models."

"I know, but I think I'd like to work with kids—help kids like Tommy—but I don't know how." Kenny's expression brightened. "You really have faith in me, don't you?"

"Of course I do. I know you can do whatever you want. You'll find a way to work with kids if that's what you want, but you need to finish your training. The force needs people who want to work with kids just as much as it needs patrol officers like Sam and your dad. So talk to them, find out what they do." Kenny smiled, and even though the room had started to cool, Bobby felt a warmth he hadn't felt before. Kenny was happy, and it was because of something he said. "Kenny, there's something I really want, but I'm scared of it."

Kenny's eyes sparkled. "You can do anything you want," he said.

"Do you mean that?" Kenny nodded. "Even this?" Bobby felt his stomach leap as he leaned forward and did something he'd wanted to for years: he kissed Kenny.

His lips felt so good and tasted even better. He wanted this so bad that it took him a second to realize that Kenny wasn't kissing him back. Then he felt an arm around his back and Kenny's lips moved. A second arm joined the first, and then he was hugged close, the pressure on his lips building as Kenny took charge.

Then Kenny pulled away, and Bobby wondered what the hell happened. "Listen," Kenny said, not moving. "Hear that?"

"Yeah, I heard it, but I thought it was my heart." Bobby saw Kenny smile for a brief second.

"I think it's coming from behind the store."

Bobby had to keep himself from swearing out loud in frustration. He was going to kill whoever had interrupted the kiss he'd waited four freakin' years for.

KENNY got up and went to the back door, listening as Bobby came up behind him. "There's someone out there, and it sounds like they're messing around with the Dumpster." Kenny turned off the alarm, unlocked the door, and peered out, gasping softly. "There's someone going through the trash." He closed and locked the door before turning to Bobby. "It looks like they're drinking the dregs from the empty wine bottles."

Kenny reopened the door to let Bobby take a look. "I think I know him," Bobby said. Kenny shut the door and Bobby rushed into the office to grab their coats with Chloe following right behind. "Stay here, girl."

Kenny opened the door, and they stepped out into the alley. A man was standing beside the Dumpster in a dirty, threadbare coat, pulling bottles out of the trash bag with one hand, the other lying limply at his side. He wiped the neck on his arm and then upended each one, sucking out any wine before throwing the empty into the dumpster with a clang.

"What do you want?" the man asked, turning and glaring at them, his eyes fearful and his hands shaking visibly.

"It's okay, Charlie. It's me... Bobby."

The sound of his own name from a stranger seemed to throw him. "Bobby? I don't know no Bobby!"

"Sure you do. You helped me a few years ago." Kenny watched as Bobby stepped closer, still talking to him. "What are you doing here, Charlie?"

The man squinted and looked through what must have been hazy eyes. "You're that runt kid that Big Mike was taking care of." There was no malice in his voice, but Kenny saw Bobby shudder. He then bent down and picked up another bottle. "I need to keep warm." Charlie's hands began shaking harder, and he dropped the bottle, smashing it on the pavement.

"I know, Charlie, I know."

Kenny whispered softly in Bobby's ear. "What's wrong with him? He's shaking like a leaf."

"He's a chronic alcoholic, and he hasn't had anything to drink. He's probably going through some sort of withdrawal." Kenny saw the sad, drawn look on Bobby's face, and he wanted to hug or kiss that look away. "Charlie, this is Kenny. He's going to stay here. I want you to put the bottles back in the Dumpster, and I'll bring you something." Kenny watched as Bobby turned to him. "I'll be right back." Bobby raced inside and Kenny watched as Charlie slowly lifted the bag, putting it back in the Dumpster. He then watched the door expectantly.

Kenny stepped away as the door opened again and Bobby re-emerged carrying a bottle in a brown bag. "Should you do that?"

"There's nothing anyone can really do for him. I'm surprised he's still alive." Bobby stepped forward slowly. "Thank you, Charlie." Bobby held out his hand, giving Charlie the bottle. "Go find someplace warm for the night."

Charlie took the bottle in his grimy hand, holding to his body like it was the best thing he'd ever received. "You were always a good boy." Kenny watched as Charlie ambled away down the alley, twisting open the bottle and drinking. Kenny felt the cold seeping through his jacket, and he knew Bobby had to be cold as well, but he didn't move until Charlie was out of sight.

"Was that really a good idea?" Kenny asked, but the sadness on Bobby's face silenced Kenny's other questions. Putting a hand on Bobby's back, he guided him back into the store and locked the door. "Let's get some dinner and go home." Bobby fastened Chloe's leash while Kenny locked up and turned off the last of the lights, setting the alarm before leaving the store. They walked to the car in silence. Kenny started it, turning the heat up full blast. "Do you really think you should have done that?"

"It was a small thing compared to what he did for me." Chloe pranced around the back seat before stepping forward and climbing on Bobby's lap, instinctively knowing he needed comfort.

"What did he do?" Kenny put the car in gear and pulled out of the parking space as snowflakes began to flutter through the headlight beams.

"He allowed Dad to find me. I was able to get away from Big Mike because Charlie stood up for me, and it cost him the use of his arm. Big Mike found me a few days later outside the store. That time Sean rescued me and gave me a home." Bobby couldn't hold back the tears. "Charlie was hurt, so I could get away." Bobby grabbed a napkin from the door pocket and wiped his eyes. "Giving him a bottle of wine's the least I can do."

"But isn't that just encouraging him?" The snow started coming down harder as Kenny navigated them through the city streets toward home.

"Charlie is so far in the bottle, nothing's going to pull him out. I hadn't expected to see him again." Bobby turned up the heat. "I just hope he's able to find someplace warm."

"You never cease to amaze me. The way you understand people blows me away."

"I've been there. I spent months on the street living with them, relying on them. I'd still be there if it wasn't for Dad." The car got quiet. The only sounds were the engine and the heater fan. "On the street, no one does something for nothing. It took me a long time to accept that Dad didn't want anything from me but to love me and be loved in return." Bobby looked out the window as snowflakes danced through the headlight beams. "I never told anyone this, but the first night Dad brought me home, I took off all my clothes and got into his bed. I owed him for his kindness, and that was the only way I thought I could repay him." Bobby smiled to himself. "I can still see the look of horror on Dad's face as he shielded his eyes and told me to get dressed and go back to my room. It was then that I started to realize that he wasn't like everyone else." Bobby took a deep breath and released it. "The only other person up till then who did something for me but didn't want anything in return, was Charlie. I wish he could stop drinking, but he can't. I think there's just too much he needs to forget."

Bobby became quiet, and Kenny left him alone with his thoughts. He concentrated on his driving, pulling up in front of the house a half hour later. "Let's get inside where it's warm."

Bobby ran a hand gently across Kenny's cheek. "I'm hoping we can pick up where we left off."

Kenny grinned wickedly. "We'll see."

"We'll see?" Bobby looked indignant.

"Maybe." Kenny's eyes gleamed as he teased.

Bobby opened the car door. "I'm going inside, and maybe I'll let you kiss me good-night." He held up a finger. "Maybe." Bobby took Chloe's leash, and Kenny watched as he hurried up the walk.

With a groan he opened his door and rushed up the walk behind him, sliding his arms around Bobby's waist. Bobby yelped and Chloe barked as they skidded to the front door.

Bobby unlocked the door with Kenny still holding his waist. Kenny pressed his lips to Bobby's ear. "Let's get inside so we can warm up," Kenny said. The door opened and Chloe rushed inside as Bobby released her leash, attacking her dish while they stripped off their coats. Then Kenny leaned forward, capturing Bobby's lips, feasting on them. This was what he'd wanted for so long. It was in his grasp, his for the taking, and he intended to take whatever Bobby was willing to give. "Thought I'd ruined this."

"How?" Bobby asked, but Kenny cut off his words with another kiss, pressing him against the wall with a thud. "That first Christmas after we started college?" Kenny nodded as his lips worked their way down Bobby's neck. "Well, we're here now, aren't we?"

"Yeah, let's get something to eat, so we can go upstairs and have dessert," Kenny suggested. Bobby nodded as Kenny pulled away. "I promise dinner will be quick and dessert will take a long time."

CHAPTER 11

BOBBY could hardly believe his ears. Kenny was going to take him upstairs, and all they had to do was make it through dinner. He followed Kenny into the kitchen, and they indeed had a very quick dinner. The excitement carried him through, but as he put his dishes in the sink, the doubts started. He'd wanted Kenny, been in love with Kenny for years, but what if he wasn't good enough? What if things didn't work out? Would he lose his best friend? He didn't know if he could bear for that to happen.

"Nothing will affect our friendship, Bobby," Kenny said. "You've been my best friend for years, and you always will be, but I want this." It was almost as if Kenny could read his mind.

Bobby whispered, "I do too." Then he felt Kenny's hand in his, tugging gently, and he found himself following automatically, his desire pulling him along, up the stairs and into his room. To Bobby's surprise, Kenny opened the door to the small airing porch and tugged Bobby out onto the balcony, the cold air biting his skin until Kenny pressed up behind him, arms pulling them close, trapping the heat between them. The night was nearly silent as white flakes drifted out of the darkness and into the light of the open door, swirling toward the white dusted ground below.

"I love nights like this: the snow falling like angel feathers, the sound of the waves as they murmur against the shore." Kenny's voice resonated in Bobby's ear as his breath blew warmly over his neck.

"This is artfully ironic, you bringing me out here into the snowy night." Maybe he shouldn't have vocalized what he was feeling, but he'd rather know now than find out later. He just hoped Kenny understood what he meant.

"Mmmm, hmmm." Kenny's breath swirled around his ears. If it weren't for the cold, Bobby would have thought he was dreaming this, but the zing told him it was real. Lips touched the back of his neck and fingers slid beneath his sweater, opening a button on his shirt. Then he felt Kenny's skin against his, a hand rubbing softly, fingers teasing their way lower.

Kenny did understand, and without thinking, Bobby stretched, his long body becoming longer, and a second hand joined the first, stroking his chest. "Kenny," Bobby moaned softly as his muscles elongated on their own, giving Kenny more access, calling out on their own for his touch. Then Kenny moved back and Bobby moved as well, drawn to him like steel to a magnet—across the threshold and into the warm room where the door seemed to close on its own. Kenny turned him around; lips touched his, hands threaded through his hair. Heat worked its way through his clothes and all his doubts evaporated and coalesced into desire.

"I've waited so long for this," Bobby said.

"How long?" Kenny's breath skimmed against his neck.

"That last night before we went away to college, I almost snuck into your room. I wanted you then, but was too scared to do anything about it." Bobby threw his head back as Kenny kissed and softly sucked on his neck, just above the shirt collar. "I've wanted you and fantasized about you since then."

Kenny pulled back. "I hope I can live up to your fantasies." Kenny pulled Bobby's sweater over his head.

"You already have." Kenny was kissing him again, maneuvering him toward the bed, and then he was tumbling and laughing as he bounced on the mattress before Kenny pinned him down, his weight feeling good and solid on top of him. "More than lived up to them." Bobby tried to open Kenny's shirt, but he couldn't think, let alone make his fingers move, as Kenny's mouth kept pummeling his, tongue thrusting, lips tugging and tasting. "Want more, Kenny, want to feel you like I have all those nights we slept together. I had to feel you through our pajamas then. Now I want nothing between us."

Kenny lifted his head and began opening Bobby's shirt, parting the fabric like a stage curtain, kissing his way along the smooth skin that revealed itself. "So smooth and hot." Lips touched and kissed his skin, leaving hot wet trails across him. Bobby squirmed as Kenny's fingers brushed over a nipple, swirling and pinching, his lips following, licking and sucking the buds to hard peaks. Bobby thrust his chest forward, mashing himself against the object of his fantasies.

"Kenny...." Bobby whined softly as his pants became exceedingly tight.

"What is it?" Kenny asked. Bobby felt a hand brush over him. "Are these pants getting a little tight?" Kenny's hands slid around his waist. Then a hand slid into Bobby's pants and over his butt, increasing the pressure even more. A hand ghosted over him, lightly skimming the front of his pants.

"Uh huh." Bobby vibrated and thrust forward as Kenny brushed over him again. "Don't tease me—I've had years to be teased. I just want to feel you." The hand on his butt slid away, and he felt fingers at the front of his pants, opening, sliding down the zipper.

Fingers brushed over his cotton-clad length. "Is this what you want?" Kenny slid Bobby's pants down his legs, and he kicked them off, gasping for breath as the fingers returned, sliding his underwear against him. The cotton was pulled down and he sprung forward, Kenny's fingers wrapping around him, sliding, gripping.

"Yeah." Bobby began thrusting into the hand, his feverish brain needing release, craving it. This was Kenny touching him, stroking him. This was his Kenny making him feel the way no one else ever had. "I'm so close." His breath hitched and his stomach tightened, his hips driving forward, trying to get that little bit of extra sensation that Kenny just wouldn't let him have. "Please, Kenny," he begged, through a lust-induced haze.

"Not yet." The fingers slipped away, and he felt Kenny's weight disappear. Bobby watched as Kenny stood next to the bed and opened the buttons of his shirt. The planes of his chest became visible as the fabric separated and slid off his shoulders, falling to the floor. Kenny's pants were next and Bobby began panting gently as Kenny lowered them, cock bouncing as he stepped back to the bed. Automatically, Bobby reached for himself, but Kenny stopped him with a touch and a shake of his head. "I've waited too—waited a long time to get you in bed like this, naked in bed, ready for me."

"All you had to do was ask." Bobby would have jumped through hoops for Kenny.

Kenny shook his head. "Wasn't ready for it yet. Wouldn't have realized how special it was unless I had something to compare it with." Then Kenny was back, lips kissing, weight pressing on his, but this time, it was skin to skin. This time he could feel Kenny against him, really feel him. A strong chest pressed against him, hands sliding over his skin, and Kenny's long, thick length pressed against his stomach. "But I'm ready now," Kenny whispered into Bobby's ear.

"Me too." Bobby was so turned on, he could barely stand it. Every time he moved, he moved against Kenny, and he felt Kenny slide against him. Bobby wrapped his legs around Kenny's waist, and he felt rough fingers slide over his skin, teasing his opening, but going no further.

Kenny kissed him again, his lips touching Bobby's, his tongue tracing the contours of Bobby's mouth before diving in full force. Bobby vibrated beneath Kenny's touch, his strong loving hands leaving quivering skin wherever they touched. He'd had lovers before, but no one had ever made him feel like this. No one had ever looked at him the way Kenny was looking at him right now.

"What do you see when you look at me like that?" Bobby asked. As Kenny's hand slid over his cheek.

Kenny swallowed hard. "I see everything I could want." Then Kenny's lips were back on his, taking him hard, plundering his mouth as hands plundered his skin. Bobby let his own hands roam free. He wanted everything all at once. There was no way he could get enough of Kenny, but as soon as fingers again teased at his entrance his wants shot out of his head.

Kenny put a finger to his lips and Bobby sucked on it, working it in his mouth. Then Kenny pulled it away with a pop before pressing the finger to his entrance, teasing the guardian muscle.

"I'm not going to last if you do that." Bobby could feel his stomach already starting to hitch.

"I don't want you to last. I want you to come so hard you see spots and your head spins." Kenny pushed deeper, sinking the finger fully before rubbing and stroking. Bobby ground against him, wanting more, but not sure he would last long enough to get it. Then Kenny brushed against that spot deep inside him, and the spots started as he felt the pressure start to build.

"Kenny!" He gasped for air as the pleasure slammed into him.

Kenny smiled. "I knew you'd like that." Then he did it again, making small circles, brushing over the spot with each pass, and Bobby felt his climax building from his fingers to his toes.

"Kenny!" Bobby could hold back no longer and his eyes crossed as he thrust forward, his cock gliding against Kenny's skin, the sensation just enough. His body shaking and breath ragged, he gasped loudly and cried out as he spilled himself between them.

"That's beautiful, so beautiful." Kenny watched him as he came down. "You're incredible when you come, you know that?" A thumb slid across Bobby's lips. "More beautiful than I imagined. Your lips tremble and your body shakes. Your eyes go all liquid and they shine like the sun."

Bobby felt Kenny's finger slip from him, and Kenny's lips came to his, the kiss filled with Kenny's unspent passion. Bobby smiled into the kiss and swung them around, looking down into Kenny's sparking eyes. "Now it's my turn."

THE sparkle in Bobby's eyes filled Kenny with passion. He'd never had someone look at him like he was the center of the world before, and it was kind of intimidating, in a hot, erotic sort of way. "Now that you've got me, what are you going to do with me?"

Bobby smiled wickedly and then leaned forward. "All those times I've seen you with your shirt off, I always wondered." Bobby's head lowered, and his lips latched onto a fleshy nipple, sucking and teasing it to hard perfection. His tongue swirled and his teeth lightly scraped.

"Jesus!" Kenny called as Bobby smiled against his chest and repeated the treatment on the other nipple, nipping lightly at Kenny's chest. "Where'd you learn that?"

Bobby shrugged and kept at it, making Kenny squirm beneath him. "You taste good."

"What do I taste like?" Kenny's head went back as Bobby's lips shifted, tongue sliding along his side, lapping at him like a big Popsicle.

"Sweet and a little salty. You smell good too, like a hot, workin' man." Bobby inhaled deeply and then blew hot air on Kenny's damp skin, making him shiver with delight. "But in order to form a better opinion...." Bobby slunk down Kenny's body, hands sliding over his skin as he found what he wanted. "I need a better taste."

Kenny groaned as he felt Bobby's tongue slide around the head of his cock, lips sliding down his length, teasing him for what he hoped was to come. "Bobby." Now it was Kenny's turn to whine and plead as Bobby took his time, savoring his length before opening his mouth and sliding his lips around the head and then slowly taking more and more of the shaft.

All of him—Bobby took all of him down his throat. Kenny wound his fingers into Bobby's hair as he came up for air and then did it again. It was so hot that Kenny was afraid the top of his head was going to blow off. Fingers softly stroked the skin of his balls, and he could feel them tightening against his body.

"Bobby...." He tried to give warning, but his climax barreled into him, and he couldn't stop it. "Bobby...." His warnings just seemed to spur Bobby on, and Kenny came in a rush, pouring himself as Bobby sucked and swallowed.

"God, Bobby." Kenny panted as he began to come down from the most intense, mind-blowing orgasm of his life. Opening his eyes, he saw Bobby smiling up at him with a very satisfied look on his face. "You blew me away." Bobby crawled back up his body and flopped on the bed next to him. Kenny rolled over and pulled his lover close. As soon as his mind registered the words, he smiled. Bobby was now his lover as well as his best friend. He liked that. "Have you had many lovers?"

Bobby shook his head. "My roommate and I slept together for about six months, but it didn't work out."

"Why not?" Kenny asked as he snuggled against Bobby's back, his hands sliding up and down Bobby's chest and stomach.

"For the same reason I could never get close to anyone... like that. They weren't you." Bobby rolled over so that he could face Kenny. "You were the one I always wanted, and no one else could measure up. I'd never even touched you, and you'd already spoiled me for anyone else. I only hoped if I waited long enough that I'd get you somehow. How about you?"

"A few, but no one really serious. I dated a guy named Clay up until a week or so ago. He was fun, but it wasn't serious, at least not for me." Kenny began nuzzling Bobby's neck, letting his tongue slide over the hot skin. "I never really thought about it, but even when I was with them, you were never far from my thoughts." Bobby rolled back over and Kenny spooned him. "I was always afraid I'd ruin our friendship if we—"

"Made love?"

"Yeah. Stupid huh?"

Bobby shook his head. "I was afraid of the same thing." Kenny felt Bobby push his butt back against him, and he felt his body react forcefully. "I want you, Kenny, want you inside me." Bobby said. He squirmed a second and then handed Kenny a condom from the nightstand.

"Are you sure?"

"Very sure."

Kenny took him at his word, maneuvering Bobby onto his back and kissing him. The thought of being inside Bobby had him throbbing and painfully hard. Reaching to the nightstand for lube, he slicked his fingers and slid first one and then another into his squirming lover.

"Relax… I need to get you ready." There was no way he was going to rush this and hurt him.

"I'm ready."

Kenny pulled out his fingers and rolled on the condom before lifting Bobby's legs and slowly sinking into him. The tightness and heat were like nothing he'd ever experienced before. He'd done this before, but never with someone so important, never with someone who meant as much to him as Bobby did. Before, it was just sex. But this, this was something completely different.

"God, Kenny, so full." Bobby's eyes locked onto his, and he started to move. Slowly his hips rocked, and Bobby's body gripped him like a vice, holding onto him like he was afraid to let go. Each time he pressed in, Bobby would moan softly, and whenever he pulled back, a long groan would fill the room.

"Love the noises you make." Kenny picked up the pace and so did the noises. They filled every corner and every crevice of the room, building into a crescendo that carried them along on the waves of their own passion. They moved together, hands gliding along skin, lips finding each other's as Kenny drove deep into Bobby.

"Take me. Make me yours, all yours."

Kenny drove deep, his climax building, and if the sounds Bobby was making were any indication, he was just as close. "Come with me, Bobby." His lover nodded his head, and Kenny changed the angle slightly. Bobby cried out, his body clenching and gripping Kenny, sending him over the edge on wings of ecstasy.

They didn't move for the longest time, each needing to catch his breath. "You're wonderful," Kenny said. Bobby gave a small sigh as Kenny felt himself slip from his lover's body.

"So are you," Bobby said, slipping from the bed and returning with a cloth and towel. After a sensual cleanup, he put them away and climbed back into bed. "You feel so good."

Kenny pulled their bodies together. "Mmm, yeah." The house was quiet and dark, only the soft night noises occasionally murmuring around them.

"You never told me, and I always wondered why you ran away from the foster home."

Bobby rolled over so he could see Kenny's face, surprised that he'd never told him, but realizing that he'd never talked about it much. "I got shuffled around after my mom gave me up. My last foster family, the McDowells, were really nice at first. They treated me like one of the family and everything, not like some castoff kid. I was there for about," Bobby stopped and thought, "I guess a couple of months when my foster brother, Greg, started making me feel uncomfortable, getting too close and touching me. I didn't think much of it at first, but he kept on even when I told him to stop."

Bobby sniffed and tried to roll away, but Kenny stopped him. "I know it's hard, but I've got you." Kenny held tight, his lips kissing Bobby's neck and moving to his ear.

Bobby continued, his voice lower and softer. "One Saturday, my foster parents were gone, and Greg and I were home alone. He began wrestling with me, pinning me to the floor. I told him to stop, but he wouldn't." Bobby sniffed and wiped away a tear before going on. "He grabbed me and began rubbing me through my clothes, and then he tried to put his hand in my pants. I wiggled away, and he jumped on me and rolled me over, pulling down my pants." Kenny tightened his arms around him, letting Bobby know he was there. "His folks came home, and I scrambled away, rushing to my room."

"Did you tell them?"

Bobby shook his head. "I ran away. I guess I figured they wouldn't believe me anyway. The people before them had sent me away when they found out I was gay, so I figured they wouldn't be any different."

"Is that how you ended up on the street?"

"Yeah. It was summer and not too bad. But then it got cold. Dad took me in about six months later."

Kenny held Bobby tight, rocking him slowly, knowing he had to comfort him. The door nudged open, and they felt Chloe jump on the bed and settle at their feet. Kenny continued comforting him as they drifted off to sleep.

Kenny woke a few hours later, Bobby sleeping peacefully next to him. He could see his relaxed, sleeping face in the soft glow from the street-lit window. Doubt and fear crept in big time, and he actually tried to slip away into his own room, but Bobby shifted, his arm tightening around Kenny's, and him snuggling his head against Kenny's shoulder. The soft, contented smile on Bobby's face was enough to get Kenny to settle back on the pillow. Bobby was happy and that made him happy. The rest they'd figure out... he hoped.

CHAPTER 12

BOBBY woke to the irritating sound of his alarm and the warm feeling of Kenny sleeping next to him. Before he realized it, his hands began to explore his lover's firm body—skin smooth over hard muscle, arms thick, hands big and strong. He knew it was time to get up, but that was the last thing he wanted to do. Once Kenny woke, Bobby had no idea how he was going to react, and he wanted very much for the magic to last. Bobby watched as Kenny's eyes fluttered open and a soft sigh rumbled in his chest.

"Morning." A smile formed on Kenny's mouth, and Bobby knew things would be okay. "You were wonderful last night." Kenny slid a finger down Bobby's nose, and after he turned on his side and propped his head on his hand he continued. "I should have known you'd be a spitfire in bed."

Bobby blushed. "No one's ever told me that before. Maybe it's you."

"I'd like to think so." Kenny leaned forward, placing a kiss on Bobby's lips. A soft whine from the foot of the bed followed by feet tramping up the covers reminded them that they had things to do and that they couldn't stay in bed all day. "I don't want to get up. I want to stay here in bed, with you."

Bobby snuggled closer. "Me too." Their lips met in a soft kiss that promised that more was to come, later. Reluctantly, Bobby slipped out of the warm bed and pulled on his robe. Chloe was already on the floor, prancing around, so Bobby trudged downstairs and let her out, returning to find Kenny already in the shower. Slipping off the robe, he opened the bathroom door and pushed back the shower curtain. Kenny's was washing his hair, his head back, rinsing his hair. "Now that's beautiful," Bobby said. Kenny's arms were raised over his head, as he stretched his strong body into a tall tower of muscle. Bobby stepped in, his hands gliding over the planes of firm skin. Soaping his hands, he slicked Kenny's skin, letting his hands roam over his lover's body.

"I like that." Kenny's voice was deep and rich, rumbling in his chest.

"I thought you would." Bobby soaped Kenny's chest and legs, purposely ignoring his now hard length. "Turn around and rinse off." Kenny complied, and Bobby washed his lover's strong back and shoulders. His hands kneaded the rippling muscles before sliding lower and gliding over the tight butt.

Bobby knelt down and let his fingers slide along Kenny's crease and between his legs, all the way to his balls, before sliding back. Kenny's legs vibrated as Bobby repeated the movement again and again. "You feel so good, Kenny." Bobby loved that Kenny was allowing him to leisurely explore. He couldn't get enough of him, and he hoped he never did. Bobby let his hands slip away, and Kenny rinsed himself under the spray.

"Your turn." They switched places and Kenny soaped his hands. "Reach up and grip the shower head."

Bobby looked down his nose, but lifted his hands, placing them around the shower pipe. He looked into Kenny's eyes, seeing a hint of mischief that turned him on. "Is this okay?"

"Perfect. I like you like this, long and lean." Kenny began washing Bobby's skin, and it was his turn to vibrate. Those hands slid and stroked, swirling around his nipples and down his stomach, before gliding down his legs. Kenny tapped his inner thighs lightly and Bobby spread his legs farther, shifting his weight and taking a wider stance. He was immediately rewarded by Kenny sliding his fingers up his crease, teasing his opening. Bobby felt his legs start to shake as Kenny leaned forward, taking him into his mouth.

"Kenny." Bobby pushed his hips forward, and Kenny took him deeper, while a finger slipped past his muscle, sliding into his body. He was caught between pleasures and he wasn't sure which one to concentrate on. When he pressed forward, Kenny took him deeper. When he backed away, the finger went deeper. He finally gave up and rocked gently, doing his best to enjoy both at the same time. "Gonna," was all he managed to say as his orgasm slammed into him hard, knocking the wind out of him as he geysered into Kenny's mouth. "Kenny, oh God, Kenny!"

"Keep hanging on." His hands on the shower were the only thing keeping him upright and then he felt Kenny's hands around him, propping him up, not letting him fall, as air heaved into his lungs again. "That was beautiful." Kenny shut off the water and opened the curtain, grabbing a towel and wrapping it around Bobby. "You were beautiful."

"But what about you?"

"The sight of you coming like that was such a turn on, I came right after you did." Kenny began rubbing Bobby down with the towel before drying himself. "We need to get going."

Bobby nodded, barely able to talk. Still in a bit of a daze, he wandered back to his room, dressing quickly before heading downstairs to let the dog in. As Bobby opened the back door, he saw Chloe sitting on the step, looking up at him as if to ask, "What took you so long?" She wandered inside before ambling into the kitchen to check out her bowl.

"We're almost late, so I'll grab something for us to eat once we get to the store," Kenny said as he entered the kitchen, encircling Bobby in a hug.

"Okay." After another kiss, Bobby got Chloe's leash and they put on their coats and left the house. It hadn't really snowed more than a dusting, but after putting Chloe in the car, they brushed it off and headed toward the store.

The windows were dark when they arrived. Kenny parked and hurried inside. The lights came on and Bobby heard the ladder being set up in the back. He figured Kenny was trying to get something done before Katie arrived. Bobby let Chloe off her leash and went to the office. It didn't take long before he had everything ready. Stepping out of the office, he heard the front door open and close.

"Morning, guys," Katie called.

"Morning, Katie," Bobby answered as Kenny scrambled out of the ceiling and put the ladder away.

"I need to get that cable," Kenny said.

"Why don't you do that when you get us something to eat? You can install it after Katie goes home. She's only working until two or three." Bobby carried the cash drawer to the register and handed it to Katie so she could open. As he approached, he noticed her rubbing her belly. "Everything okay?"

Katie took the cash drawer from him. "He's kicking today."

"Yeah?" Bobby's interest was piqued. "Can I feel?" Bobby smiled as Katie guided his hand to her belly, and sure enough he could feel movement inside. "Cool." His eyes were wide with wonder. "Stan must be about ready to burst with pride."

Katie looked askance. "Oh, he is." She got to work opening the register. "Sometimes I despair of all of you. He walks around with his chest all puffed up, like 'look what I did.'" She actually growled at Bobby. "All he did was have one of his little swimmers get lucky. I'm the one with stretch marks and a bladder that's shrunk to the size of a pea."

Bobby stopped what he was doing and stared at her, not having a clue what to say. He nearly threw up his hands in surrender.

"Sorry, my hormones have been running rampant for days. This morning I actually cried because the Danish wasn't cherry, and

I'm the one who bought them." Katie wiped her eyes. "Jesus Christ!"

Bobby handed her a tissue. "You okay?"

"I'll be fine." She blew her nose and then threw the tissue away. Bobby unlocked the front door, and since the store was quiet, Bobby used the opportunity to disappear in the back for a while.

Kenny was again on the ladder. "I'm almost done. As soon as I get the cable and hook it up, we'll be all set."

"Good." Bobby stepped on the bottom rung, running his hands over Kenny's tight butt.

"What are you doing?" Kenny took a step down the ladder.

"That should be quite obvious," Bobby said, smiling. Kenny looked through the stockroom door to the sales floor. "Katie isn't going to care if I'm feeling you up."

"Bobby." Kenny stepped down, and Bobby climbed off the lower rung to let him get down. "Are you sure this is a good idea?" Damn, he'd never seen Bobby's face fall so quickly. "I didn't mean that I'm sorry about last night. I'm just concerned what Katie, Sean, and Sam are going to say about this—about us."

"I think they'll be happy for us." Bobby stepped back as Kenny reached for him. "You need to make up your mind about what you want. Last night you told me all those wonderful things, and today you're all, 'I'm not sure.'" Bobby walked toward the sales floor door and turned. "When you grow a pair, let me know!" Bobby let the door swing closed before Kenny could say anything. He then stormed to the office, picked up his sketchbook, and did what he always did when he was upset: draw.

KENNY watched Bobby's back as he stalked into the office. He knew what he was doing. For as long as he'd known him, whenever

Bobby was upset he did two things: withdraw and pick up his sketchpad. Kenny wanted to try to explain, but now wasn't the time. He needed to let Bobby cool down. With a sigh, he glanced at the office door before putting the ladder away and checking out the sales floor.

There were a few customers in the store, but it was otherwise pretty quiet. He figured now would be a good time to get the cable he needed, and he was about to grab his coat when he saw through the windows a large, familiar car pull up. He smiled and headed out front to greet Mrs. Gold. She was getting out of her car, and he walked outside to meet her, Sean's best customer and quite a lady.

"Kenny." She smiled as he took her hand, holding it in his. "How have you been? I understand that Sean and Sam are somewhere warm."

"They're on a cruise," he said as he escorted her into the store.

She looked around expectantly. "Sean told me that you and Bobby were looking after things."

"Bobby's in the office, drawing."

She wandered through the store, picking up a few bottles before stepping to the counter and setting her purse on it. Opening the bag, she pulled out a piece of paper. "I have a list of things I'll need for this weekend." Sarah Gold was one of Milwaukee's premier hostesses, and she entertained for her husband on a very regular basis. For years, she'd been a loyal customer of Sommelier Wines. "Can I pick them up Wednesday?"

Kenny scanned the list. "The store is usually closed on Wednesdays, but I don't see why not. Let me get it together. Or would you rather we deliver it?"

"Would you? I could send someone, but with two parties in as many days, everyone's so busy."

"It's no problem. I'll call you when we have everything and arrange for delivery. We'll be glad to do it." Kenny looked back toward the office. "Would you excuse me a minute?" She inclined her head, and Kenny walked to the back room and into the office. Bobby was sitting on the futon, legs drawn up, sketchpad resting on his knees, pencil flying. "Bobby." Kenny waited and when he didn't respond, he spoke up. "Bobby, Mrs. Gold is here and I thought you'd like to see her." Kenny sat down next to him as Bobby's legs straightened, and he put down the sketchpad. "I didn't mean to upset you, and I wasn't expressing regret, just concern."

Bobby's big eyes looked so... sad. "I thought you regretted what we did last night." The way Bobby said the words left Kenny feeling that so much was being left unsaid, and he wanted to ask about it, but now wasn't the time.

"I didn't, I don't. I just... I'm not sure what I meant, other than to express concern about how people might react. Most everyone thinks of us as brothers and—" Kenny let his thought trail off. "Come on, we can talk later." Getting up, he extended his hand and helped Bobby to his feet.

"Bobby!" Mrs. Gold called as he approached, and Kenny saw the look of unabashed delight on her face. She and Kenny had always gotten along, but she and Bobby had a special connection, something they'd always had for as long as Kenny could remember. "How's my favorite artist?" She gave him a hug, which was something she only did with Bobby. "How's school?"

"Good." Even from where he was standing he could see Bobby was being evasive.

She narrowed her eyes. "Don't give me any crap, what's going on?"

Bobby heaved a sigh. "I have to do a senior project to graduate and nothing's coming. Everyone expects something brilliant and I don't have any ideas." Kenny approached and stood next to Bobby, putting his hand on his back without even thinking about it. "Sometimes I think something's close, but it slips away again."

"What did your advisor say?"

"That I needed to look deeper into myself. That I needed to find that part of myself that I was keeping locked away, whatever that means."

She took him by both hands. "When you did the piece for the airport, you expressed what you were feeling at the time, and it came through in the work for everyone to see. That's why you were chosen. You need to find that same source of emotion and find out where it comes from."

"But I don't know how."

"I don't know either, but this I do know. When you find it, you'll know it, and you won't have any doubt."

They got quiet, so Kenny added. "And it'll happen when you least expect it."

Sarah smiled. "Listen to him. He's right. The more you worry or try to force it, the farther away it'll feel." She let her hands slip from Bobby's. "I have to get back. I'll expect to see both of you when you deliver the wine." She hugged Bobby, and to Kenny's surprise, she hugged him too, a knowing look on her face that he didn't understand. With a wave to Katie, she walked out the door and climbed into her car, driving away. Kenny couldn't help thinking that Katie called her the Zephyr, because she always blew in and out of the store like the wind, and Katie was right.

Kenny reached into his pocket and handed Bobby Sarah's list. "Would you call this in?" Bobby nodded. "I'm going to get some things completed, and then we can go get the video cable."

"Sure. Meet me in the office in half an hour and we'll go."

"Okay." Kenny got to work while Bobby left to arrange for delivery from the supplier. When the displays were full, he met Bobby in the office, where they got their coats. "Katie, we need to run an errand, we shouldn't be too long."

She leaned against the counter, the store devoid of customers at the moment. "No problem." She waved as they left the store and drove to Radio Shack.

Kenny used the time in the car for them to talk. "I meant what I said earlier. I don't regret what happened last night." He reached over and squeezed Bobby's leg. "I've wanted to be with you for a long time."

"Me too, and I guess I never thought it would happen," Bobby said, putting his hand on top of Kenny's. "When it did, I was afraid it was some sort of dream that was too good to be true." Kenny smiled as he drove, pulling into the parking lot.

"It's not a dream, so we need to enjoy it." Bobby nodded and Kenny kissed him before getting out of the car. "I'm not ashamed of you or how I feel about you," Kenny said, holding the door for Bobby. "Let's get this cable so we can figure out what's happening at the store. Give ourselves one less thing to worry about."

CHAPTER 13

BOBBY didn't say much on the way back to the store. Kenny's words were running through his head. He knew Kenny was trying to reassure him, but there was so much Kenny hadn't said, and Bobby was kicking himself because he hadn't pressed. But it was becoming clearer to him that Kenny seemed to view what was happening between them as temporary, and Bobby didn't know how he felt about that. He knew he wanted something permanent with Kenny, he always had, but could he walk away with his heart intact if Kenny decided he wanted to walk away? Bobby didn't know, and that was the source of the fear.

A touch on his leg pulled him out of his thoughts. "Are you okay? You looked like you were mulling over the fate of the world."

Just the fate of my heart. "I'm fine." Bobby forced himself to smile through the butterflies in his stomach and think of something else. "How long will it take you to hook up the camera?"

"Not more than an hour. I just have to connect the cable and set up the equipment to record without showing that camera on the monitors."

"I hate this, Kenny. I hate suspecting Katie and Laura. When I saw her this morning, I kept wondering if she was stealing from Dad. Katie's been with him since the store opening. He trusts her, and we should be able to trust her."

"Do you want to stop and let whoever's stealing from Dad get away with it?" The look on Kenny's face made Bobby shiver. His eyes were suddenly so cold and hard. Bobby shook his head. "I didn't think so."

Bobby turned in the seat. "That doesn't mean I have to like it, does it? I feel like we're spying on people. People I care about, people who've taken care of me, of us, people who love us." Bobby could feel himself getting upset again, but he couldn't help it.

"I know how you feel." Kenny's slipped a hand into Bobby's. "I really do. What I'm truly hoping is that we can prove it isn't any of them. That something else altogether is going on. What, I have no idea, but I don't want it to be them either." They pulled up to the store and got out of the car, carrying in their purchase. "Hey, Katie, everything okay?" All traces of his earlier concern were gone, and Bobby wondered if Kenny was turning his feelings for him on and off the same way. The very idea made him suddenly feel cold.

"Everything's fine." She got down off her stool behind the counter and wandered over. "You weren't gone very long." She looked down at the bag but didn't ask what was in it, which Bobby thought was a little unusual. But he was grateful they didn't have to come up with a lie.

"We didn't want to leave you here alone for very long in case it got busy, so we hurried."

Kenny walked to the back, leaving Bobby with Katie. "If you bring out some stock, I can put it away. I just can't lift the cases." The store was quiet, and since they might as well keep busy, Bobby brought out some of the extra stock as well as a stack of promotional wine to fill the tasting area. Bobby set the refill cases near the areas where they'd be needed and got to work. "The cabernet you brought out a few days ago is great. I wish we had some more. We're down to the last case."

Bobby wished the same thing. There would have been more if a case hadn't gone missing. "I thought it was pretty good." No matter how much Sean had tried to teach him about wine, Bobby just didn't really get it. He liked it well enough, but he never did taste all those things that Sean and Katie always said they could. He brought over the last of it from the tasting area so Katie could work it into the general display, and he began rebuilding the special display.

"What's Kenny doing?" She looked briefly toward the door and then went back to her task.

Bobby shrugged and kept working. He wasn't a very good liar, so he figured the best thing to do was plead ignorance. A few minutes later Kenny joined them. "Would you bring out the last three cases of the Red Lion chardonnay?" Bobby asked, showing Kenny the wine in question. Kenny returned with the cases and Bobby added them to the display. "All set?" he whispered as Kenny helped him with the cases.

"Yes. It's all hooked up and working perfectly." Kenny cut one of the cases for display while Bobby cut the other, removing a bottle and adding it to the tasting area. At least none of these cases had gone missing. "I've got it recording now, even though there should be nothing. I don't want to take any chances."

"Would it be okay if I worked in the office for a little while?"

"Sure, go ahead. I'll stay out here. Are you feeling the urge to draw?" Bobby nodded. "Then go ahead. We can handle things for a while."

"Thanks, call me if you need me." Bobby began walking toward the back, and he heard Kenny laugh.

"Not that you'll hear us."

Bobby made a motion like he'd been wounded. "Thanks, Kenny." But he knew it was probably true. If he got engrossed in something, he probably wouldn't hear them. Walking into the office, he settled on the futon with his sketchpad with Chloe joining him, curling up next to him. Bobby scratched her coat for a few minutes and then began to draw, becoming lost in the images in his mind. At first they were all scattered and jumbled, but he waited and they slowly coalesced into an expression of what he was feeling. Last night he and Kenny had made love for the first time. Pushing aside his doubts and worries, he concentrated on what he'd felt the night before, recalling the passion and excitement, the fulfillment of years of dreams. With a smile, the image firmed, and he began to draw.

His lover's eyes shone back at him as Bobby transferred Kenny's expression as he came onto the paper, followed by the way his lip curled slightly, the slight flush of his cheeks, the furrow of his brow, and mussed, just-loved hair. Bobby set the pad on the table and looked at the finished drawing. Too bad he couldn't turn that in for his final project. "I don't think my professors would appreciate that, do you, Chloe?" She lifted her head and huffed before lowering her chin back to the cushion. 'I didn't think so." Bobby picked up the pad and slipped to a fresh page and began another.

The images kept coming, and he went with them, putting each of them on paper without censoring or even thinking. It was a great feeling. The juices were flowing again. Every piece didn't have to be some sort of masterpiece. Every drawing didn't have to be perfect. Expressing what he was feeling was good enough. The rest would take care of itself. He wasn't sure if that was the long-term answer, but it was working, so he didn't question it.

"How's it coming?" Bobby looked up and saw Kenny standing in the doorway, smiling brightly. "Looks like you got something done." Kenny sat next to him, and Chloe jumped down, looking a little put out before wandering out front.

"I did." He flipped through the pad and showed Kenny the drawings.

"Is that how you see me?" Kenny stopped him with a touch of his hand as he stared at the drawing of himself.

"It's how you looked last night." Bobby suddenly felt apprehensive. As he looked at it now, he saw how raw and open the drawing was. It left no doubt whatsoever as to what they'd been doing and how Bobby felt about Kenny. He'd laid his emotions bare in that drawing, and what if Kenny rejected it—and him? Bobby watched, but Kenny said nothing, just starting at the drawing with his mouth open.

KENNY could hardly believe his eyes—Bobby loved him. After seeing that drawing, there was absolutely no doubt. He could have shouted it at the top of his voice, and it wouldn't have had the impact of that drawing. He moved his eyes, looking to Bobby, but his attention was inexplicably drawn back to the drawing. Looking at it, he could feel the way he'd felt the night before. He could feel the heart-swelling moment when Bobby made him feel like he was the most important person on earth, all because Bobby was with him and only him. He could feel that moment when everything in his brain became tingly, and his vision fuzzed that split second before Bobby brought him over the edge. "Bobby." He could see through his own eyes staring back at him, how much Bobby wanted him. "Do you really feel like that?"

"Like what, Kenny?" Bobby locked his eyes onto Kenny's. "You have to say it."

Kenny looked stricken for a second. "Say what? That I can see you love me?" Kenny got up and started pacing across the office floor. "Your drawing makes that very plain. I've known that you loved me since we were kids. It was that love that got me through my dad's death and his funeral and got me through the rest of high school without going crazy. That picture doesn't say that you love me, it says that you're in love with me." Kenny stopped pacing. "You're in love with me."

Bobby nodded softly. "Yes. I love you, Kenny, have for a long time. At first I didn't realize that's what I was feeling. When I did, we were already away at school. That first Christmas, I was about to tell you how I felt when you…" Bobby swallowed and Kenny could see that he was trying to keep his emotions under control.

"When I kicked you away."

"Yeah. But you didn't know."

"Yes, I did." Kenny took one of Bobby's hands in his. "I pushed you away because I was scared of my feelings for you. Everyone I love has died. First my mom, then my dad. I know it's stupid, but I didn't want you to die too, so I pushed you away."

"But it didn't work any better for you than it did for me."

"No. I kept comparing everyone I met to you, and they just couldn't measure up." Bobby's laugh caught Kenny by surprise. "That's funny?" Bobby shook his head and started laughing harder. "You going to enlighten me?" Kenny asked. Bobby nodded as he started to get himself under control.

"I was stupid. I was willing to go to the same college you went to, so I could be near you, and when you wouldn't let me, I thought you didn't want me to be with you."

Kenny folded his hands in front of body. "Then why are you laughing?"

"Because we're quite a pair."

Kenny started to chuckle himself. "I suppose we are, but what I said before still goes. We were both too young to know what we really wanted." Noise was starting to filter in from the store, and they both got to their feet. "We can talk about this later. We've got work to do."

"Okay."

Kenny led them to the sales floor, stopping in the door. "The lesson from this is that we need to talk to one another. So I'll start. I love you, too, Bobby." Kenny took Bobby's face in his hands and kissed him hard. "We'll talk about this when we get home."

"Talk."

"Yeah, the best kind of talking. The kind where you get to use your hands." Kenny felt Bobby shiver against him, and then they both got to work.

At about three, Katie said her good-byes and left the store. Bobby spent the afternoon helping customers and confirming the delivery the next day of the wine for Mrs. Gold, while Kenny checked out the camera feed between customers.

"Still working?" Bobby's eyes glinted with mischief. "I mean, it hasn't stopped working in the last five minutes, has it?"

"Okay, I guess. I'm just anxious to find out what's going on."

"I know, but hovering won't help. You might go check the stockroom and see if anything's missing, I printed out a case inventory this morning. It's on the desk. I've been running a random check in the mornings trying to catch if something sprouts legs."

"Okay, I can do that." Kenny smiled as Bobby let his hand brush gently against his leg as he passed. "Hey, Chloe, you wanna help?" She got up from her cushion and followed Kenny into the back room. There weren't a lot of cases in the back, since the next shipment was to arrive tomorrow along with their special order. Kenny picked up the inventory and did a quick check against the cases in the back. Everything appeared to be normal with nothing missing. When he was done, he found Bobby checking out customers. "This is dumb. We're chasing our tails over this."

"I know," Bobby said, getting an empty case and packing up a customer's purchases. "Thank you. Do you need help getting this to your car?"

"No, I'm good. Thank you." The customer lifted the case and carried it out of the store.

"You're welcome and have a great night." Bobby completed the transaction and secured the register before turning to Kenny. "I hate to say this, but I hope whoever's doing this, does it again soon."

"I know." Kenny looked around the bright store. "I'm going to fill displays. I need something to keep me busy."

"Until what?"

"Until I can get you home." Kenny was really looking forward to a night of closing the store and getting Bobby into bed. "There are so many things I want to do, and all of them are designed to make you moan and scream."

"Thank God I'm behind the counter." Kenny leaned over and looked down, smiling at the bulge in Bobby's pants. Then he looked up and smiled. But the clouded look on Bobby's face made Kenny look toward the door. A tall man in an old coat stood in the doorway, his hands in his pockets, eyes down at the floor.

"Bobby, who's that?" Kenny said as Chloe began to growl at their feet.

"Call Jerry." The slightly panicked touch to Bobby's voice had him concerned. "That's my father." Kenny picked up the phone as the man stepped forward.

"Bobby, I won't hurt you. I just wanted to see you and tell you I'm sorry." Kenny looked to Bobby, the phone still in his hand, as the man spoke. "I got out a few weeks ago. I had a lot of time to think while I was in prison. I got sober and I found something that helps me."

"Where are you living?" Bobby asked. Kenny could see the insecurity in him and moved closer, touching his back.

"At a shelter downtown." The man didn't step forward, but Kenny kept the phone in his hand. "I just wanted to make sure you were okay."

"The last time I saw you, you tried to kidnap me." Damn, Kenny could hear the pain in Bobby's voice, and it went right to his heart. He knew about Bobby's past, but seeing him talking to his father brought all the unhappiness from Bobby's early childhood into focus and his first reaction was to protect him.

"I know. I wasn't well and I thought they were trying to take you away." He stepped back as he talked. "I don't want anything from you. I just wanted to see that you were okay." He left the store, turning just before he did. "But you're better than okay. You grew into a man anyone would be proud of." Then he was gone.

Kenny put his arms around Bobby just in time for him to collapse against him. "It's all right, Bobby. It's okay."

"I know. I just didn't think I'd ever see him again." Kenny kept quiet and let him talk. "But he was right there. He didn't feel threatening or anything. It's like finding out the monster under your bed really doesn't exist."

"We've got a few more hours and we can go home." Kenny gave him a hug and then stepped away.

Bobby seemed to get control of himself again. "Yeah. We can talk then." There were customers in the store, and they turned their attention to them.

CHAPTER 14

BOBBY found himself sitting behind the counter, shaking like a leaf. He couldn't believe he was reacting this way. He hadn't seen his father since the day he'd tried to abduct Bobby and Sean had whacked him on the head with a bottle of wine. And now he was back, but this time, he wasn't a scared, frightened kid, so why did he feel like one?

A hand slid along his shoulders, pulling him out of his thoughts. "You okay?" Kenny asked. Bobby shook his head. "Why don't you take a break in the office for a while? I can watch things out here."

Without thinking or noticing anything around him, Bobby wandered back to the office, plopping himself on the futon, with Chloe taking the opportunity to jump up next to him. Picking up his sketchpad, he began to draw.

"The store's locked up and the lights are out." The words knocked Bobby out of the creative haze that surrounded him. He blinked as he looked up at Kenny's smiling face. "Did you work through what you were feeling?"

Bobby nodded as he looked down at his sketchpad, filled with images of his father. Some were from when he was homeless and knew the man as Big Mike, and some were how he saw him today.

"You need to talk to him, you know." Bobby felt his gut wrench, and he shook his head vigorously. "Yes you do," Kenny said, sitting next to him. "You need to find him, talk to him, and ask him all the questions you always wished you could ask." Bobby stared back at his best friend, his lover, in stunned silence. "I always thought I had the worst luck, but I was wrong. I was lucky. I lost my dad at fifteen. He was taken from me by a criminal with a gun."

Bobby interrupted a little impatiently. "I know."

Kenny continued as though Bobby hadn't spoken. "But he didn't leave me, and I know without a doubt that he loved me and that he arranged for caring, loving people to take of me. You never had that, and you never knew that. You deserve that too. You deserve the answers to all your questions."

Bobby looked into Kenny's eyes. Was this what he'd been missing? His instructors had told him to unlock the part of himself he'd kept hidden away. Was this it?

"I don't know what you're thinking," Kenny continued, "but I know one thing. You won't find the answer you're looking for tonight. At least not all of it." Kenny held out his hand and pulled Bobby to his feet. "Let's get you home and into bed. I made you a promise earlier, and it's one I intend to keep." Kenny grabbed Chloe's leash from the desk. "Come on, girl, it's time to go." Fastening the lead onto her collar, Kenny led both Bobby and Chloe out of the store and into the car. They arrived at the house with Bobby not even remembering the drive. Kenny opened the car doors and Bobby followed him into the house, still lost in his thoughts and worries.

"Bobby." He looked up and found himself in the hall. "You going to take your coat off?"

"No, I thought I'd keep it on," Bobby replied sarcastically, as Kenny stepped close to him and slipped his coat off his shoulders, pinning his arms to his side.

"Then you're going to pay." Bobby looked into Kenny's eyes and the sinking feeling in his stomach subsided, replaced with a flutter when he saw the deep, longing look in Kenny's eyes just before their lips met. "Tonight you're mine. Say it."

"Yours." Bobby's stomach fluttered again, and he realized he was painfully hard. He shifted his hips, trying to get himself more comfortable.

"Tonight it's all about you. Your job is to feel. That's all you do." Kenny kissed him again, pressing Bobby against the wall. "You can tell me what you want. You can ask for what you think you want. But all you get to do is feel. Can you do that?" Bobby nodded in response as the lips were back against his, pummeling, tongue-fucking his mouth.

Then Kenny stepped away, looking him up and down while Bobby breathed like he'd just run a marathon. "I love it when you have that just-kissed look." Kenny ran his finger over Bobby's lip. "Go upstairs and undress. Lie on your back on my bed and wait for me. I'll be up in five minutes." Bobby didn't move, just looked at Kenny in surprise. "Go!" His voice had an edge that Bobby had never heard before, and it turned him on.

Bobby found himself running up the stairs, twisting and shrugging off his coat as he went. Hurrying into Kenny's room, his shirt hit the floor, shoes thunking as he toed them off. Pants followed along with his socks. Naked, he climbed on the bed, lying on his back as instructed and waiting for Kenny. After what seemed like a lot longer than five minutes, Kenny appeared in the doorway, shirtless and barefoot, wearing only a pair of tight leather pants. He looked hot as hell as he prowled toward the bed. "My beautiful baby, I'm going to make you scream my name." Kenny stalked to the closet and pulled out what looked like two ties. "Do you trust me, Bobby?" He nodded. "You have to say it."

Bobby thought for a split second. "Yes, I trust you." Even during those years they hadn't been speaking, if Bobby had been asked that question, he would have replied the same way. Trust was never the issue.

"Put your hands over your head." Bobby complied and then slippery material slid across his wrists. "The only hands I want touching you are mine." The silken tie tightened around his wrists. "These aren't really tight, and you can pull your hands free if you want." Bobby shivered as Kenny ran his fingers lightly down Bobby's arm. "You like that?" Bobby nodded again. "You can talk, Bobby. In fact, I want you to." Kenny slid a hand over Bobby's chest, taking a nipple between two fingers.

Bobby hissed between clenched teeth as Kenny lightly pinched a nipple. "Yes, I like that."

"Then you'll really like this." Kenny reached beneath the bed and showed Bobby a pair of gloves. "These are mink." Bobby watched, eyes wide, as Kenny put one of them on. "These are really soft." The fur glided over his skin, making each of his nerve endings scream with delight. He smiled as the fur slid over his chest, moaned softly when it glided over his thighs, and groaned deeply when Kenny took his balls in his gloved hand.

"Kenny." The gloved hand twisted along his length and he thrust involuntarily into it before it slipped away. "Do that again! Please!" Bobby's voice was shaky with need.

"What?" Kenny's look was pure deviltry. "This?" A gloved finger slid along his length.

"Yes, Kenny. That!"

"All in good time." Kenny walked around the bed, settling between Bobby's legs, sliding the glove along his thighs. "Lift your legs... higher... yeah, that's it!" Kenny slid the glove over Bobby's butt as he leaned closer, swiping his tongue along Bobby's crease.

Bobby went nuts, trembling as he felt the first touch of that hot tongue against his skin. "Kenny!"

"Has anyone ever done this to you before?"

Bobby's head rocked against the pillow. "No."

Kenny lifted his head, eyes locking on Bobby's. "Then it's about time." Then his head disappeared and the tongue reappeared against his skin before slipping away again. "Keep your legs up."

Bobby complied as he watched Kenny open the front of his pants and slip them down his legs. "You promised me, Kenny."

Bobby heard a packet rip open. "I always keep my promises." The bed shifted and then Kenny was there, looking into his eyes again as he pressed forward, entering his body. "Always." As Kenny sank into him, the fur glove began sliding along his skin.

Kenny began moving, sliding against his gland with every stroke. The gloved hand wrapped around Bobby's length, pulling and teasing as they moved together, Kenny filling him exquisitely. Bobby had never felt anything like this. His nerves were firing, spots flashing behind his eyes, as he thrust into Kenny's fur encased hand. "Kenny!"

"Come on, Bobby, let it go. Give me everything." Bobby cried out as his climax overtook him, painting white ribbons on his stomach as he heard Kenny crying out his own release.

KENNY felt good, and Bobby felt good next to him. The room was cool, but Bobby was hot, like Kenny's own private furnace pumping heat right next to him. He didn't want to get up—didn't want the contented feeling to end. He could hear his lover's soft breathing and the occasional snort that he soon realized came from Chloe, curled at Bobby's feet. What was he going to do? He'd always loved Bobby, but over the past few days, his best friend had wormed his wonderful way into his heart, and Kenny knew there was no going back. What he'd told Bobby was true: he did love him. But in less than a week, he and Bobby had to go back to school.

Who knew what was in store for them? What if Bobby found someone else? How would he deal with that after the last few days? The answer came to him quickly, and he knew he'd be heartbroken.

Just thinking about it made his insides quiver a little. Last night during their lovemaking, Bobby had told him he trusted him. Kenny reminded himself that he trusted Bobby, and that included trusting Bobby with his heart.

"Kenny." Bobby's big eyes blinked open, and he moved closer, curling their bodies together. A soft groan from the foot of the bed served to remind them both that they were disturbing her majesty's beauty sleep. "Go back to sleep."

"I will."

"Your mind keeping you awake?"

"Yeah, I guess."

"Don't worry… won't hurt you." Bobby yawned as he put his head next to Kenny's on the pillow.

"I know, but what if I hurt you?"

Bobby shifted next to him, propping his head on his hand. "If that's the worst of your worries, then I think both our hearts are in good hands." Bobby leaned forward to kiss him. "Whatever happens, we'll figure it out."

From Kenny's experience, things were rarely that easy, but now was not the time to discuss it. Snuggling together, he let himself drift off to sleep.

"KENNY." A soft rocking of his shoulders disturbed his sleep. "We need to go." Bobby was already dressed.

"Why didn't you wake me earlier?"

"You looked so peaceful, I didn't want to disturb you. Get cleaned up, I have breakfast for you, and then we need to go. Stan called, and he'll be at the store with the delivery in forty-five minutes.

Kenny threw back the covers and rushed to the bathroom, only to have Bobby stop him by grabbing his butt. "I thought you were in a hurry." His body showed definite interest in what Bobby's hands were doing at that moment.

"We always have time for a kiss." Bobby got what he wanted as Kenny pressed him back on the bed, tempted to forget about the store and get Bobby naked. But he pulled away and hurried to the bathroom, closing the door on Bobby's temptation.

Kenny cleaned up and dressed quickly, meeting Bobby in the kitchen. He grabbed a quick bite before he, Bobby, and Chloe left the house.

By some miracle, they managed to beat Stan to the store. But they'd no sooner turned on the lights when they saw him pull up. "Morning, 'Dad'," Bobby called, and they saw Stan puff with pride.

"You guys ready?" His smile was huge. "I've got plenty on the truck for you, including the special order from yesterday."

Kenny kept yawning, so Bobby answered, to Kenny's gratitude. "We'll meet you around back."

Stan left the store and Kenny locked the front door, joining Bobby in the back. Stan unloaded the truck, Bobby checked the cases, and Kenny moved them into the store, with Chloe supervising the entire process. Half an hour later, the doors were closed and Bobby had signed the delivery paperwork. "Did Sean leave any instructions on what he wanted where?"

"I think so. I'll go get it while you set aside the cases for Mrs. Gold." Bobby went to the office while Kenny neatly stacked the ten cases they were to deliver tomorrow. Bobby approached as he worked. "Dad says that most of this is for tasting promotions for the rest of the week and weekend. He got a deal on the Rolling Hills Riesling," Bobby patted the cases in question. "So he has a special he wants to run."

"Then we need to rework the tasting display and get this on sale." Kenny began transferring the Riesling to a cart. "We may as well get started before the store opens."

"Okay, you bring out the wine and I'll start reworking the display." Bobby didn't step away, and Kenny used the opportunity to steal a quick kiss before returning to work.

Kenny finished loading the cases and wheeled them to the sales floor only to find Bobby staring at the dismantled display. "It looks like the Red Lion was more popular than I thought. There's just under five cases left."

Kenny crinkled his brow. "I don't remember selling that much of it." Kenny got a weird feeling. "Run a sales report and see how many bottles we actually sold."

Bobby was already moving. "You don't think...?" Bobby's voice trailed off as he left the sales floor. Kenny counted the remaining bottles and checked the tasting records.

"We started with ninety-six bottles and used three for tasting." Kenny spoke loudly so Bobby could gear him throughout the store. He heard the printer and then a rip.

"The report indicated we sold twenty-one bottles."

"So there should be seventy left. I count fifty nine. Eleven bottles missing—not even a full case." Kenny banged his hand on one of the cases in frustration. "What the hell is going on here?" Kenny felt his temper blaze. "Employees be damned! Friends be damned! The only people who could have done this are the ones who work for us!" In class he'd learned about victims and how they felt, but he never expected to feel that way himself. He now understood firsthand the feeling of frustration and helplessness that were described in his classes.

"Kenny, calm down, please." Bobby backed away at Kenny's display of temper.

But Kenny couldn't. His temper was up, way up. "We're going to find who's doing this, and I'm going to nail them to the wall!"

"Kenny, I know how you feel, but this isn't helping!" Bobby's frustration sparked Kenny's protective instincts, cutting through his own.

"I'm sorry. You're right. This isn't helping. Let's get this done, and then we're going to talk over everything we know and figure this out." Kenny got to work, his body stiff, movements forced as he worked out his anger and resentment.

Bobby nodded his agreement, and they worked quietly, getting the display reworked and the excess wine returned to the stock room. Bobby then spent time organizing and counting the cases in stock, making sure they were all full and sealed before returning to the office. "We have half an hour before the store opens."

Kenny looked up from the security monitors. "It's going to take some time to go through all the cameras, but I haven't seen anything so far."

"Let's talk it through and maybe we'll get an idea of what to start looking for." Kenny pushed back from the desk and joined Bobby on the futon. Chloe, who'd been furtively following them all morning, jumped up as well, curling up at the far edge of the futon, like she could feel the tension. "The first case disappeared before Dad left, so we don't know much about that."

"No. But when the Coppola was taken, Katie wasn't here, and Jimmy wasn't here. The only one who had been here was Laura, but she hasn't been in since we put out the Chardonnay. So she couldn't have had anything to do with that and Jimmy hasn't been in either." Kenny picked up the schedule from the desk. "He doesn't work until tonight."

Bobby got up and started to pace. "So where does that leave us? The bottles didn't walk out the door, not that many in two days. Besides, why would someone take that many bottles of one particular wine?" Bobby began to think, pacing from one side of the office to another. "There's another possibility." Kenny watched as Bobby's eyes began to dance. "Oh God, this is good."

"What? What is it you're thinking?" Kenny could feel himself becoming anxious.

"Have you ever read *Murder on the Orient Express*?"

Kenny crinkled his brow. "No, why?"

"Let's get the store opened." Bobby left the office, and Kenny watched his bouncy steps as he followed him to open the store, wondering what in hell he was thinking.

Chapter 15

"YOU really think this is going to work?" Kenny walked to the counter where Bobby had just finished helping a customer.

Bobby shrugged as he looked toward the back of the store where Katie had disappeared for what seemed like the eighty-seventh time that day. In her words, "I'm not only eating for two, but peeing for two as well."

"I don't really know, but it won't hurt anything," Bobby said, moving in closer. "All we need to do is stay out here and review the video of the back room after we close."

"I suppose so."

"What are you two talking about, looking so cozy?" Bobby looked up and saw Katie waddling across the sales floor. She seemed to get bigger every day.

"Guy stuff." Bobby retorted a little too quickly, but he didn't want her asking a lot of questions.

"Don't give me that crap." She walked over and sat on the stool next to Bobby. "Spill it."

"I was just telling him that I think he should talk to his father." Kenny reached into his pocket. "He's got unresolved issues, and I think he really needs to talk to him. Ask the questions he's always wanted answers to."

Bobby huffed. "I don't have questions I want answers to." His eyes were blazing.

Katie touched Bobby's sleeve. "I've known you since Sean rescued you almost seven years ago, so don't try to pull the wool over my eyes. I know the thought of being in the same room with that man scared the hell out of you. But you must have questions. Don't you want to know why?"

"Of course I want to know why." Bobby blurted as his temper got the best of him. "Of course I want to know why he was never part of my life, not that it really matters. Not that he'd have been any better than my mother. What does it say about me? My mother abandoned me because her drugs were more important, and my father was a raving drunk who couldn't think past his next bottle of booze!"

"Bobby," Katie said, keeping her voice level, "that says a lot about them, but nothing about you, absolutely nothing at all."

Kenny pulled a scrap of paper out of his pocket and handed it to Bobby. "I had Jerry do some checking for me, and he was able to find where your father's staying." Bobby opened the paper and stared at the address written on it. "It's a mission downtown. According to his parole officer, that's where he's been sleeping since he got out of prison."

Bobby refolded the paper and jammed it back into Kenny's hand. "I don't want it. I never want to see him again for as long as I live."

A few customers came in and began looking around, and Kenny got up to help them, slipping the scrap of paper into Bobby's pocket. "Just hang on to it, and think about it." He stepped away before Bobby could argue, but then returned. "I'd give anything to be able to ask my dad a few last questions. You have that chance, so think about it." Before Bobby could loose the nasty retort on the tip of his tongue, Kenny was already off to help the customers.

Katie rested against the counter, looking at Bobby. "You really should think about it." Bobby glared at her as she continued. "He's only trying to help because he cares about you."

"I know." Bobby sighed quietly. "I just don't want to—"

"Deal with it?" Katie supplied. "You need to deal with it once and for all." Patting Bobby's hand, she got up from the stool and went to help some customers who'd just entered the store.

Bobby sat behind the counter, not really seeing what was going on, letting his mind run. The thought of seeing his father again turned his insides. When he'd been in the store, he'd been too surprised to be scared, but now that he'd had time to think, he'd also had time to worry. When he thought of his father, he instantly felt fear. This was the man who'd attacked him behind this very store. This was the man who'd stalked him and tried to abduct him on more than one occasion.

He looked up. "Kenny," Bobby said, once he'd finished ringing up a sale and thanking his customer. "If I go see him, will you go with me?"

Kenny looked surprised. "When I told you to see him, I most certainly didn't mean for you to go alone. Of course I'll go with you." Kenny ran his hand down Bobby's arm. They were in the store, so overt displays of affection weren't appropriate, but Bobby understood what Kenny was telling him, and he felt a warm feeling spread from inside. Kenny was there for him.

"Hey, guys." Bobby jumped and turned toward the familiar voice. "Sean told us you were manning the store for him, and we thought we'd drop by to see how you're doing." Mark was smiling at both of them, Tyler right behind him. Before they could answer, they were both engulfed in hugs, first from one and then the other. Tyler asked Kenny about some wine and the two of them walked toward the display at the front of the store. "So how's your work coming?"

"All right."

"Just all right? What gives?"

"I have to come up with a senior project. All my ideas don't seem to work or aren't good enough. Because of my past success, they expect me to deliver some sort of masterpiece and nothing's coming. My professors tell me that I need to dig deeper; Kenny thinks I need to resolve things with my father; and I just don't know what the fuck to do." Bobby realized he was talking too loudly and looked around before lowering his voice. "Every time I think something's coming, it vanishes in thin air." He knew he was whining a little, well maybe a lot, but he also knew that Mark was the one person who would understand exactly what he was going through.

"We all have this happen to us at one time or another."

"But everyone keeps telling me different things I need to do."

"No, they're not. I think they're all telling you the same thing in a different way. You're just not listening." That got Bobby's attention. "Your professors expect a lot from you because they know you're capable of it. So does Kenny, and so do I. And maybe, just maybe, Kenny and your professors are telling you the same thing. Maybe digging deep inside yourself and your feelings about your father are linked together."

"How do you know?"

"I don't. Only you do. But you never will unless you explore it. Part of being a good artist is doing good work. Part of being a great artist is doing good work and infusing it with your deepest and most powerful emotions and feelings. People may not like what you're showing them, but they can't help being moved by it, and that's what makes art great. Not how pretty the picture is, or how well it's executed, but the feeling behind it. Great art will always impart some sort of emotion, but you can't produce it if you're afraid to explore *your* emotions."

"So what do I do?"

"Chase after what you fear most, and don't be afraid to explore the emotions that are hardest. Love and hate are easy to deal with, but try expressing your fear, sadness, regret, jealousies, and everything else. Then it gets hard, because each time you do that, you're giving others a glimpse of your soul." Bobby listened intently. "Go see your father and ask him what you want to ask. Yell at him, scream at him, hit him if you want to, but when you're done, channel what you're feeling into your work. See if that doesn't break your block." Bobby watched as Mark stepped away, joining Kenny and Tyler.

AFTER a long day, Kenny finally turned the lock in the front door, closing the store. After Mark and Tyler's visit, Bobby had acted different, and he'd even agreed to try to visit his father at the mission after they delivered Mrs. Gold's wine tomorrow morning.

"Kenny! Kenny!" Bobby practically screamed with delight from the stock room. "There's a case missing!" Kenny shook his head as he smiled. He never thought he'd hear Bobby be happy to find a case of wine missing. "It worked."

"So what do we do now, Sherlock Holmes?" Kenny approached the stockroom door as Bobby was coming out to meet him, the two of them practically colliding into each other.

"Well, we—meaning you—need to review the footage from the camera in the stock area for the last few hours. The missing case was there at six."

"How do you know?"

Bobby grinned, "Because I arranged the cases in an artistic pattern that I could recognize and now the pattern's been disturbed, and I can't find the missing case of Monkey Business." He led toward the office, fidgeting as Kenny sat at the computer and recalled the video.

"Monkey Business?"

Bobby began to chuckle. "That's the name of the wine."

"This could take awhile." Kenny started the video and an image of the stockroom appeared. "That's the case that's missing just keep your eye there." Bobby pointed and Kenny nodded as he sped up the playback.

The recalled images flew by with very little to see. Bobby walked through on his way to the office and Kenny laughed as he looked like he was running. Then Bobby returned and Kenny came through looking like he was moving to some punk beat. They both laughed as the image settled down and nothing changed. The frames flew by, minute after minute, with no change.

"Stop it," Bobby said a little loudly in Kenny's ear, and he paused the playback. "There's something going on in the corner. Play it at normal speed." Kenny reduced the speed and the video slowed to normal. "See, it's Jimmy." They watched as he walked into the frame, looking around. Then he picked up the case in question and carried it toward the office, going inside. A minute or two later he emerged again without the case of wine. After looking around again, he picked up the broom and left the stock room.

Kenny stopped the video and looked at Bobby. "What the hell? So it was Jimmy."

"You're missing the point. The missing case has to be in here."

"But it was Jimmy all along?"

Bobby grinned again and shook his head. "No. *Murder on the Orient Express.*"

"What in hell is that supposed to mean?" Kenny was completely confused.

"Didn't you Google it?" Kenny shook his head, so Bobby continued. "*Murder on the Orient Express* is the quintessential 'they all done it' story. With the exception of Poirot, everyone's guilty."

"So you're saying?"

"Let's find the wine." Bobby began rummaging through the office, looking under the desk, behind the filing cabinet, and in the closet. Chloe, thinking it was a game, began running around the office, jumping on top of and trying to slink beneath the futon before backing away. Kenny watched as Bobby got on his hands and knees and began looking around the floor. "Kenny, help me lift the futon."

"You're crazy." Kenny took one side and Bobby took the other lifting it up and into the center of the room. On the floor were three cases of wine: the Bollinger, the pinot, and the newly missing case from the stock room. "So, umm, what's your theory Sherlock?"

"I think Dad hid the Bollinger, Laura hid the Pinot, and as you know, Jimmy hid the last case."

"If you're so smart, where are the missing bottles of Chardonnay?"

"Wherever Katie put them." Bobby crinkled his brow and pulled away what looked like something sticking out of the case of Bollinger. "It's an envelope." Bobby opened it and pulled out what looked like a single piece of paper. "It's a note… from Dad."

"What's it say?"

Bobby began reading. "Boys, sorry for the small bit of subterfuge, but I thought a little mystery might get you two working together again. Laura, Katie, and Jimmy were only doing what I asked them to do. You used to be the best of friends, and I'm hoping working together to solve the mystery will bring you two closer together. Tell me all about it when I get home. Dad. P.S. If it didn't work, act like it did."

Kenny stared at Bobby completely dumbfounded as he watched him fold the paper and put it back in the envelope. As he stared, Bobby's face broke into a smile and then he started laughing. Soon his laughs turned into guffaws and he held his side. "What's so funny? Sean tricked us."

Bobby nodded and tried to speak, but couldn't. "Yes... he... did." Bobby continued laughing. "We can tell Dad it worked." Bobby continued laughing. "Better than he ever dreamed."

Kenny finally got it and started laughing himself. "God, he's gonna swallow his teeth when we tell him just how well his little trick worked." They continued laughing, settling on the futon, with Chloe jumping and barking excitedly.

They eventually got themselves under control. "So what do we tell everyone?" Kenny asked.

Bobby raised his eyebrows. "Nothing at all. Those three are going to be dying for us to figure it out. So we'll say nothing and let the three of them pay for having their part in this."

"Okay, I get it," Kenny said as they got up and lifted the futon back into place, leaving the wine just where they'd found it. "What if more goes missing?"

"They'll start to run out of places to put it." Bobby started laughing again. "We'll act completely oblivious and let them have their fun." After a look around to make sure everything was back in place, Bobby scooped up the envelope from the desk and turned off the office lights. "Let's go home. I'm a little tired."

Kenny looked down his nose, imitating a look he often got from Bobby. "Does that mean you're *too* tired?"

"Are you kidding? I just need some food and then I'm all yours for the whole night."

Kenny switched off the lights before slipping his arms around Bobby's waist. "I like the sound of that." Bobby arched as Kenny ghosted his lips against Bobby's neck. "Lucky for both of us the store is closed tomorrow, and we don't have to get up," Kenny added. Bobby started to laugh, and Kenny said, "I said we don't have to get up. Getting *it* up is a given." Kenny slipped his hands beneath Bobby's shirt, rubbing lightly over his lover's stomach and chest. "Let's get us some food so we both have plenty of energy."

"Yeah, let's," Bobby said as he groaned softly when Kenny slipped his hands away. Getting Chloe's leash, Kenny fastened it on her collar, and after locking the door they headed for the car. "I'm worried, Kenny."

"About tomorrow and seeing your father?" Kenny had a feeling that was still bothering Bobby.

"Yeah." Bobby told him what he wanted as Kenny pulled into a drive-thru. "I just can't help being nervous about it."

Kenny pulled forward and they got their food. "After we eat, I'm taking you upstairs, and I can promise you that for a few hours, you'll forget all about it." Kenny saw Bobby shiver a little as they pulled back into traffic and toward home. He had every intention of making sure Bobby was too tired to think about anything other than him until well into the morning.

CHAPTER 16

THE car pulled away from Mrs. Gold's huge, Italianate, palazzo-style home. "Jesus, I knew she was rich...."

Kenny smiled and whistled. "Yeah, but to be that loaded...."

The home was spectacular, what they'd seen of it. To their disappointment, Mrs. Gold wasn't home, so they'd left the wine with one of the staff and then driven out of the stone-paved circular drive and back out to the street.

"Where to now?" Bobby looked sheepishly over at Kenny, hoping he'd forgotten.

"You know very well where we're going. You promised you'd talk to your father, and I intend to hold you to it." *Damn, Kenny always remembered everything.* "If you remember, you got your incentive for that agreement last night." Bobby remembered, boy did he remember. "And if you're good...." Kenny's eyebrows lifted, but he said no more, guiding the car through downtown traffic and then out to the west side of town.

As they drove, brewery buildings, now converted to lofts, gave way to single-family homes, which gave way to more homes with chain link fences, and then to shabby homes some with missing windows, here and there a burned-out shell.

Bobby remembered this neighborhood. He'd lived here with his mother in a duplex that had a leaky roof and a bunch of older kids downstairs. At the time, he hadn't understood what all the comings and goings below them meant. Now he knew and he suspected those same kids were responsible for enabling his mother's habit. "I don't want to be here."

A hand squeezed his leg reassuringly. "I know you don't. Look, Bobby, I'll turn the car around, and we can go home if that's what you *really* want to do."

Bobby could hear the tinge of disappointment in Kenny's voice, and he could feel it himself. It was time he girded it up and did what he needed to do. "No. We're doing this. I'm not going to chicken out." He said the words with more confidence than he felt, but it helped anyway.

"Good." Kenny pulled the car into a parking space in front of an old storefront and put the car in park. "We're here."

Bobby peered out the window and shivered. "I know this place. I used to get meals here sometimes." Bobby pulled the latch and opened the car door, slamming it behind him to cover his sigh. He let his eyes wander up the front of the weathered building to the cross that adorned the front. Bobby heard Kenny walking around the car, his footsteps crunching on the sidewalk.

"Let's go inside."

Taking a deep breath, Bobby walked to the front door and pulled it open. The first thing that hit him was the smell: unwashed bodies combined with lingering food smells and the scent of the building's decay. Stepping inside, Bobby took a few steps, and the door slammed behind them.

"Can I help you boys?" A tall, broad man walked toward them in jeans and a black shirt with a Roman collar. "Lunch won't be served for half an hour."

"We're not here to eat, Father George." Bobby recognized him from all those years ago. He looked older, but he still had the energy he remembered. "We're looking for Big Mike."

The Father's eyes narrowed. "He's been working hard to turn his life around."

Kenny put his hands up in a gesture of conciliation. "We're not here to cause trouble. Bobby's his son and he wants to talk to him."

The priest's eyes narrowed again as he studied Bobby hard. "I remember you, but it's been a long time. I wondered what happened to you."

Bobby smiled for the first time in hours. "It's a long story, but suffice it to say, I met someone very special who took me in, gave me a home, and adopted me. I'll graduate from college in a few months."

The smile he got from the priest couldn't have been happier or warmer. "Well, I'll be damned." The man shook his head. "Talk about a happy ending." The light in his eyes dimmed slightly. "We don't get many of those here." He changed the subject. "Mike's in the kitchen, helping make lunch. I'll take you through." The priest turned and Bobby followed, glad Kenny was with him as they walked down the corridor to the dining room.

It had been painted since Bobby was here last, but other than that, everything looked the same. With each step, Bobby could almost feel himself traveling back through time, and it wasn't pleasant. The room, the sounds, the smell—all worked to bring back memories he'd just as soon have left forgotten. "Mike, there's a young man here to see you." Father George motioned for them to have a seat, and a few minutes later, Bobby saw his father, the man he'd known on the street as Big Mike, walk into the room and stop when he saw Bobby. "Mike, your son came to see you."

The tall man nodded and slowly stepped forward. Father George walked to him. "It's okay. I'll stay if you like." He shook his head and the priest moved away. Bobby was sure he'd be close by.

"I didn't expect to see you again." Mike pulled out a chair and slowly sat down, moving almost meekly. Bobby hardly recognized him as the same man who'd at first protected him and then tried to possess him. "Not after what I done."

Bobby didn't know where to begin. "I don't want to talk about that other than to say that I forgive you, because if you hadn't done what you did, I wouldn't have met Sean. He's given me a loving home and a good life." Bobby knew he was bragging slightly, but he wasn't sorry. Sean had given him a better life than he could ever have expected.

"I know. I saw you in the papers when I was in prison." A cup of coffee materialized in front of each of them and Bobby saw Mike wrap his hands around the mug to give them something to do. Once Father George had left the room again, he continued. "I was messed up for a long time." Bobby watched as the older man's eyes seemed to gloss over. "After you were born, I tried to stay clean and dry but that didn't last long. Your mom pushed me to the curb and did her best to raise you on her own. From what I know, she did good for a long time." Bobby nodded.

"Do you know what happened?" Bobby had always wondered why his once fun-loving mother had turned into the addict he knew later.

"No. I think the pressures got to her after awhile."

"I always wondered if this would be different, if I'd—"

"None of it was your fault," Mike said, cutting him off. "Not what happened to your mom or what I done to you. The fault was hers and mine, but not yours." Mike looked up and they saw Father George walk in. "He helped get it through my fat head that no one else is responsible for me but me."

Silent as a ghost, Father George appeared at their table. "I need to open the doors for lunch."

Mike got up slowly, hanging on to the back of the folding chair. "I got cleaned up in prison, and I've worked hard to stay that way. Father George helped a lot." Bobby had to admit, he barely knew the meek, quiet person standing in front of him. He seemed so different from the Big Mike he'd known.

The sound of feet shuffling down the hall signaled that it was time for them to go. Bobby saw Father George and thanked him as the first people entered the dining hall. "Is there anything we can do?" The words were out before Bobby even realized he'd said them.

"We always need help." The smile on the priest's face was radiant. Bobby and Kenny followed him and soon they were on the line serving up food. There were even a few faces he remembered.

"There're so many kids," Kenny whispered into Bobby's ear.

"Yeah, I know. I used to be one of them." Bobby continued dishing up food as his eyes wandered around the room.

"Why aren't they in school?" Kenny wondered out loud as he continued serving. "By the grace of God...."

Bobby heard the phrase and it touched something, something he hadn't thought about for quite a while. He was very lucky. He knew many of these people were here through no fault of their own.

The flood of people slowed to a trickle, and the last few were served. The tables throughout the room filled, and conversation and laughter swirled around the room.

As he looked, Bobby saw Charlie enter the room, looking a little better than he had a few days earlier, but not much. He picked up a tray and went through the line, not noticing anyone or anything. At the end of the line, Bobby watched as Charlie shuffled across the floor and sat next to his father, who appeared to help him get seated and even helped steady him, so he could eat. Bobby couldn't help smiling he saw the two of them together. That, more than anything else, told him what he needed to know.

"Thank you for your help," Father George said, coming up behind them and shaking Kenny's hand. When he turned to Bobby, he shook his hand as well and added, "I hope you found what you came for."

"I found something, but I'm not sure it's what I was hoping to get."

The priest smiled cryptically. "Maybe you'll discover you found more than you expected after all."

Bobby chuckled. "Maybe." He weaved his way through the tables and into the corridor making his way toward the front door. Bobby had to admit that he'd been expecting to find the man who attacked him as opposed to the almost broken man he'd talked to.

"Are you glad you came?" Kenny asked.

Bobby nodded and smiled. "Yes, I really am. You were right. It helped. Even if I never see him again, my last memory of my father will not be of him attacking me in an alley."

Kenny opened and held the door as they stepped into the early spring sunshine. "Then it was definitely worth it."

"Yes, it was."

Kenny unlocked the car, and they climbed inside. Bobby leaned across the seat, angling for a kiss. "Thank you for being so insistent." He was grateful when Kenny didn't respond other than to kiss him back.

KENNY drove back to the house, stopping on the way to run through a drive-thru for some lunch. They'd spent a few hours feeding others, but they hadn't stopped to eat themselves.

Pulling up to the house, Bobby raced inside to let Chloe out, and Kenny brought up the rear, carrying the food. Once inside, he brought the bags to the table and grabbed a couple plates. He was just finishing up when he heard the back door close and feet ascend the stairs, followed by nails clicking on the floor. "Lunch is ready."

Kenny sat down with Bobby across from him, smiling. God, he loved to see Bobby smile like that. "I was really surprised to see the number of kids and babies there."

Bobby took a bite of his burger. "Hunger knows no age limits." Bobby said through his food and then stopped to swallow.

"I know, they taught us that in criminal justice. But it's different when you see it firsthand. Really puts faces to the statistics you get in class."

"I guess it does." Bobby continued eating, and Kenny could tell he was starting to get lost in his thoughts. Bobby had that look about him he always got when his artist's eye was starting to get the better of him. Kenny watched as Bobby began to eat automatically, his eyes and attention were definitely elsewhere.

"Are you done?" At Kenny's voice, Bobby seemed to snap back to the present and Kenny cleared the dishes, putting them in the sink.

"So what are you doing for the rest of the day?" Bobby asked, pushing back his chair.

Kenny returned from the sink, sliding his arms around Bobby's waist, grinding himself against his lover's tight butt. "You." That earned him a low moan that increased as he nibbled on Bobby's ear.

"You are, huh?" The vibrations and shivers running along Bobby's body belied his true feelings, regardless of his words.

"Oh, yeah!" Kenny slid his hands beneath Bobby's shirt, stroking the warm skin. Bobby began to giggle and Kenny increased the sweet torture as Bobby tried to still the hands. "No, Bobby, put your hands above your head." Bobby complied slowly and Kenny ground himself against his lover's butt while his hands continued their wanderings. "Gonna make you cry out for me." Kenny's hands kept up their lazy wanderings even as he lifted Bobby's shirt. "Gonna make you forget everything but me and you, make you feel so good."

Kenny ghosted his lips over the back of Bobby's neck just before he slipped the shirt up and over Bobby's head, leaving it tangled in his arms. "Kenny, help me."

"Leave it there. I want your hands out of the way." Kenny helped Bobby out of the kitchen and up the stairs, tumbling him onto the bed. Bobby was squirming beneath him, hands still tangled in his own shirt. "I really like you like this." Kenny licked a long strip of skin across Bobby's chest as his lover squirmed. "You're all hard for me, aren't you?"

"Yeah." Bobby's hips bucked to accentuate his point.

Kenny ran his tongue up Bobby's throat and over his chin before taking his mouth, hard, possessively, communicating that Bobby was his. Bobby tried to remove his hands from the shirt, but Kenny grabbed them and held them against the bedding as he continued to pummel his mouth. "No, Bobby. Do I need to tie your hands?"

Bobby's eyes shone back at him and Kenny grabbed the old neckties he now kept in the bedside stand, fastening Bobby's hands to the headboard. "You have control everywhere else, but here in my bed, I'm in control." Kenny felt Bobby shake slightly and Kenny knew the effect his words had on his dearest-friend-turned-lover.

Once Bobby's hands were secure, Kenny worked his way lower, unfastening Bobby's pants and sliding down the zipper one tooth at a time, making sure his hands slid gently against the length pressing at the fabric from inside.

"Lift your hips." Bobby complied and Kenny pulled off the pants, leaving them bunched around Bobby's ankles as he worked off his shoes. Then the socks, pants, and underwear were gone, giving Kenny an unobstructed view. "My beautiful Love." Kenny ran his hands over the acres of skin beneath him. Kenny was about to reach for the fur glove Bobby liked so much, but he changed his mind. He wanted to feel Bobby, wanted it to be just him—no toys, just him. He wanted to be the one who drove Bobby wild.

Stepping back, he pulled off his shirt and slipped off his pants as Bobby's big eyes watched him. That intense gaze was hot. He could almost feel those eyes boring into him, watching every move he made. "You're beautiful, too, Kenny. Beautiful and strong."

A naked Kenny crawled back on the bed, his weight pressing Bobby into the mattress as their lips met again. He could feel Bobby's hips thrusting against him. "Stop moving, Love. You'll come when I want you to, so relax and enjoy." Bobby nodded and his hips stilled as Kenny continued his kissing and petting. Bobby moaned softly when Kenny sucked gently on his collarbone, raising a small mark and then licking the skin.

Kenny kissed and nibbled his way down Bobby's body, licking meandering trails across his smooth skin. At the belly button, Kenny swirled his tongue, making Bobby giggle and hiss at the same time before following the light trail lower.

The head of Bobby's cock glistened as Kenny slid his tongue over it, the taste of Bobby exploding in his mouth. "Kenny!"

"I know. You want more, and I'll give it to you... eventually." Kenny smiled as he ran his tongue along Bobby's length, bathing his balls before moving back up, sucking Bobby into his mouth, relishing the taste of his lover. Slowly, he took more and more of him, Bobby's small groans and whimpers telling Kenny all he needed to know. He loved the sounds Bobby made, and he hoped those sounds would only ever be made just for him.

Kenny took him deep as Bobby thrashed on the bed, trying to drive himself even deeper. "Kenny."

"Not yet, Love." Kenny pulled away, letting Bobby's cock slap against his skin. He leaned to the nightstand, pulling out the supplies.

"Yes!" Bobby lifted his legs, and Kenny smiled to himself. His lover was definitely eager and ready for him. Kenny tapped Bobby's legs back down, and Bobby gasped when Kenny rolled the condom down his length. "Are you sure?" he asked. Kenny nodded as he prepared himself and then lowered himself onto Bobby.

Bobby whimpered softly as Kenny took him deep inside, settling his butt against Bobby's hips. Kenny leaned forward, kissing Bobby hard before lifting and lowering himself. Bobby went nuts beneath him, driving his hips up and then lowering them to the bed. "Kenny, let me use my hands."

Kenny loosened the ties and Bobby lowered his hands, sliding them along Kenny's thighs as he drove up. "Good God," Kenny uttered. Bobby was like a man possessed. Kenny liked to be in control, but Bobby was quickly driving him to distraction, stripping away the control he thought he wanted.

"Being loved beats being in control," Bobby said.

Kenny nodded and Bobby pulled out and pushed him back on the mattress before driving back into his body. Kenny had rarely allowed someone to possess him this way, but with Bobby it felt right, natural, like he could trust him. Bobby's lips found his and they flew together. "You said you were going to make me scream, but you're the one who's going to yell." Bobby changed angles and drove deep. Kenny saw stars as sensations singed through him.

"Bobby!" Kenny did in fact yell, loudly, as his climax overtook him. Bobby cried out as well and pushed deep into him as they both came in a blinding rush.

Kenny felt Bobby pull away, and then he was back, covers pulled over them, Bobby holding him tight. "See, Kenny, when you love someone, you don't have to always be in control."

The late afternoon sun still glowed through the windows as he dozed off with Bobby holding him close. His dozing turned to full on sleep and when he woke, Kenny found himself alone. Getting out of bed, he pulled on a robe and began wandering through the house. He found Bobby in the living room curled under a blanket on the sofa, sketchpad on his knees and papers strewn around the floor.

Chloe had curled herself next to his legs and neither of them noticed when he entered the room and sat in one of the large chairs.

Kenny glanced at the papers on the floor. There were faces and hands—rough sketches and ideas taking shape. Bobby didn't look up or turn as he peeled off a page from his pad and set it near one of the others before starting to draw again. Kenny got up and went back upstairs to dress. He hoped this meant Bobby had found his inspiration, and he chuckled to himself when he realized that if Bobby had, it meant he was going to be running the store alone for the rest of the week, regardless of whether Bobby was physically there or not. He also realized he didn't mind in the least.

CHAPTER 17

"GRANDMA, Grandpa!" Bobby cried as he ran to the door of the store after seeing them through the windows. Turning the lock, he opened the door and let them in, getting hugs from both of them. "Kenny's in the back." Bobby stepped back. "Hey, Kenny! Look who's here."

Bobby continued grinning as Kenny came out from the back, striding through the store, where he too was hugged within an inch of his life. "Sean told us you were watching the store, so we figured if we wanted to see you, we'd better come down here." Their grandmother was overflowing with joy. "I knew you boys wouldn't be eating right, so I brought you some breakfast." She held up a casserole dish in a hot pack, and they followed her to the office, where she got plates from Sean's desk and began dishing up.

Their grandfather took the lull as an opportunity. "So, have you figured out what you're doing after graduation?"

Bobby looked at Kenny expectantly, waiting for him to go first. "I'm still deciding. I want to help people, but I'm not sure I want to be a police officer. I'm thinking of working with kids." He took a plate and began eating.

"How about you, Bobby?" His grandmother handed him a plate and fork.

He took the food gratefully, smiling at both his grandparents. "My advisor wants me to go on for my master's in fine arts, but I can't quite decide if that's what I want to do." Bobby began eating and Kenny used the opportunity to put his two cents in.

"I think he should go for it."

Bobby sputtered, but one look from his grandmother, and he decided not to try talking with his mouth full. Swallowing hard, he managed to choke out. "I haven't decided, but I need to make a decision soon." They continued eating, with Kenny going back for seconds and eventually thirds.

"Do they feed you at all?" Sylvia asked, as she dished up another helping for Kenny.

Kenny smiled and smelled the food. "Not like this." Kenny began eating again and Sean's mother smiled from ear to ear.

"When do you have to go back?" Howard asked, as he set his plate aside.

"I need to be back for Monday, but Bobby doesn't have to be back for another week."

Bobby smiled. "I'll be up for a day next week, and we can run the trains together." Bobby and his grandfather had spent many hours over the years playing with Howard's model trains. Bobby had painted the walls of the basement with urban landscapes and mountain scenes that served as backdrops. "I even have some ideas for a new scene on the west wall."

Howard beamed. "I thought you might."

They heard the front door open and close, then Katie's voice rang through the store and Bobby answered, "We're back here."

Katie waddled in a minute later, with both Sylvia and Howard greeting her warmly. "Sit down, dear. Would you like something to eat?"

Katie's eyes glazed over. "Are you kidding?" She grinned as Sylvia handed her a plate. "I'm eating for two." Bobby wondered how many times she'd use that excuse during the course of her pregnancy.

Bobby got up and kissed his grandmother on the cheek. "I have to open up." Kenny got up as well, but Bobby shook his head. "I'll see them next week—you visit." Bobby left the office and got the register ready for opening.

"Have we sold out of the Coppola?" Katie stopped at the tasting display, looking it over.

"It looks like it." They'd sold the four cases that had been on display, but Bobby knew that another case rested beneath the futon in the office and that this was Katie's way of trying to find out if he and Kenny had figured out about the missing wine. "It sold pretty quickly. I sure wish we could get a few more cases, but I already checked and there's none available," That ought to get her thinking.

"I sure wish I could get a case of it. Stan really liked it, and it would make a great birthday present for him." How obvious could she get?

"Sorry." Bobby finished with the register and went to open the store.

"Bobby." He heard his grandmother's voice and saw both her and Howard emerge from the back room as he walked toward them. "We've got to be going, but we'll see you next week." He hugged her goodbye, and she whispered something in his ear. It sounded like "take care of each other," but he really wasn't sure. When he stepped back, she winked at him and then headed out to their car. Confused, Bobby looked to Kenny, who grinned back at him.

Bobby watched as they got in the car, waving goodbye before pulling out of their parking place. "They're something else," he said.

"They sure are." Kenny was so close that Bobby could feel his breath on his neck.

"Did she say something to you?" Bobby asked, turning to face Kenny and peeking toward the counter to make sure Katie wasn't listening in on their conversation. She didn't appear to be.

"She told me to take care of you."

"Is that all she said?"

Kenny nodded. "I got the impression she's got the idea that there's something going on between us."

Bobby lowered his voice. "I didn't say anything to her."

"I didn't think you did. I also got the impression from her wide smile and the way her eyes twinkled that she thinks it's a good idea, but that's just an impression. Why?"

"Because I thought she whispered something to me, and it seems I heard her right. She told me the same thing about you." Bobby looked around, and since Katie was busy straightening bags under the counter, he gave Kenny a quick kiss before going back to work.

Bobby worked for the rest of the morning, cleaning the store and helping customers. Just before lunch, the phone rang. Normally, he'd let Katie answer it, but the poor thing had just left to make her one hourly potty trip, muttering something about the size of a pea. "Sommelier Wines."

"Yes, I was wondering if Kenny was there." The voice was deep, rich, and extremely sexy.

"Yes, he is. Can I tell him who it is?"

The man's voice wrapped around him again, unsettling Bobby for some reason. "Clay."

"Just a minute." Bobby put the phone on hold and walked to the stockroom, sticking his head inside. "Kenny, there's a Clay on the phone for you." Bobby saw the strange look that briefly passed over Kenny's face as he put down the case of wine and walked to the office. "I'll give you some privacy." Bobby left the office and saw Katie heading back out front.

Bobby found himself nervously wandering the stockroom. He'd never thought of himself as jealous before, but he could tell by the tone of voice that this Clay still had designs on Kenny. And Bobby didn't like it. He wanted to go back into the office and tell this Clay character to keep his sexy voice away from his lover. "Damn it."

"What are you swearing about?" Kenny breathed in his ear.

Bobby jumped and then twirled around, looking Kenny in the eye. "Who's this Clay creep?" Had he actually said that out loud? *Shit.*

"He's my recent ex-boyfriend. I told you about him the other day. I think he wanted to get back together, but I told him I wasn't really interested."

"Oh." The feelings of jealousy didn't dissipate at all. They only intensified when he realized that Kenny's going back to school meant that he'd be closer to this Clay ex-boyfriend guy.

"You're jealous, aren't you?" Kenny seemed pleased about that for some reason.

"Maybe." Bobby tried to act cool but failed miserably.

"It's over. We were never that serious anyway." Bobby knew Kenny was only trying to reassure him.

"O-okay."

"Don't worry about Clay." Kenny kissed him quickly. "Why don't you go into the office and work for a while. I'll order some lunch and call you when it gets here." Kenny pushed him gently toward the office, lightly grabbing his butt and smiling at him. He really wanted to believe Kenny, and though he wasn't completely convinced, Bobby trusted him.

KENNY couldn't believe that Bobby was jealous. As he walked back onto the sales floor, he actually smiled to himself. It meant that Bobby cared enough to be jealous, not that he had anything to be jealous of, but it was sort of nice anyway. He spent much of the morning doing regular chores around the store and trying to keep out of Katie's way, but he wasn't having much luck. She was on a fishing expedition, and Kenny wasn't biting. He and Bobby had just finished their lunch, and he could see her getting ready for her next assault when he heard the front door jingle and saw Bernice walk into the store with Tommy close behind her.

"Hi." Kenny greeted them.

Bernice walked straight up to him with a smile on her face. "We don't want to take up much of your time, but we wanted to stop in and thank you again."

Tommy stood quietly fidgeting next to his mother. Kenny turned his attention to him. "Are you doing okay now, Tommy?"

He nodded and then looked up at Kenny. "Yeah."

Kenny crouched in front of him. "Why did you run away?"

He looked up at his mother and she nodded, nudging him slightly. "Mom and Dad were fighting a lot, and I thought they didn't love me." Kenny got the feeling there was something else. Tommy glanced up at his mother and then back at Kenny.

"Why don't we let your mom shop? I know Bobby would like to see you too. He's in the office." Kenny pointed. "It's just through that door." Tommy looked at him strangely. "I'll be right behind you." Tommy walked away and Bernice seemed to breathe a sigh of relief.

"His father and I have been arguing a lot lately, but we talked and worked out a number of things, but there's something going on at school, and he won't tell us."

"Maybe he'll tell us."

"He's been talking about how nice you were ever since you brought him home. If you can find out, I'll be really grateful." It was obvious she was worried and down to her last hope. "I know you don't know me from Adam, and I don't really know you, but that police officer stopped by and told us just how much you did for

Tommy. I'll do anything to help him." The desperation in her voice jumped up a notch.

"I'll ask him and see if he'll tell us." Kenny smiled at her and walked back toward the office. As he approached, he heard Bobby and Tommy talking. It seemed that Bobby had already gotten the floodgates to open, because Tommy was talking about some kid named Bruce and the things he was doing at school to him and some of the other kids. Kenny didn't interrupt. Instead, he went back out front. "It seems he's telling Bobby his life's story. We'll give them a few minutes." Bernice seemed relieved and began browsing through the store, making a few selections and putting them on the counter.

Tommy joined her a few minutes later with Bobby following along behind him. "Mom, when we get home, can I talk to you?"

Kenny had never seen a more relieved look on a mother's face in his life. "Sure you can, honey." She hugged him and then paid for her purchases, mouthing a thank you to both of them as she pulled out her credit card.

Bobby completed the transaction and then spoke to Tommy. "Remember what I told you."

Tommy smiled and waved. "I will."

Kenny waited until they'd left the store to satisfy his curiosity. "What was the problem?"

"Tommy's got himself a bully. He picks on a lot of the smaller kids, but Tommy says he picks on him the most."

"What you tell him to do?"

"I told him to talk to his mother. She could help." Bobby bit his lower lip and Kenny had to resist the impulse to kiss it. "I hope what I told him was the right thing."

"It was. Schools have a zero-tolerance policy for that type of thing, and she really can help." Kenny turned and went back to work, dusting the displays and cleaning the racks when he heard a shriek and then one that answered. Turning around he saw Bobby hugging another man.

"Raphael!"

So this was Bobby's roommate and ex-boyfriend. Kenny looked the young, lithe man up and down. Jesus, he was really a cute little number.

"What are you doing here? I thought you were in New York," Bobby exclaimed.

"I just got back, and I had to come to town for a job interview, so I thought I'd stop in and see how you were doing. Besides, I missed you." Raphael pulled Bobby into another hug. God, they were physical. Kenny coughed softly and got Bobby's attention.

"Sorry. Raphael, this is Kenny." They shook hands and Bobby immediately turned and began talking to Raphael, the two of them going on about all kinds of things that Kenny could barely understand. Finally, Bobby caught his breath. "I think I figured out what to do for my senior project."

"Show me!" Raphael had just as much energy as Bobby did, and the two of them disappeared into the back room, laughing and jabbering as they walked.

"Jesus." Kenny sighed as he watched them go. He thought about trailing after them but decided he wouldn't understand half of what they were saying anyway.

"What's wrong, Kenny?" Katie stood next to him.

"I think I just got ditched."

Katie began laughing. "No, you didn't." She continued laughing. "Well, maybe you did. But they're talking art and school."

"I know." Kenny walked away, feeling sorry for himself. Bobby had this whole world that he wasn't a part of, couldn't be a part of. Laughter drifted in from the office and Kenny wandered back to see what was going on. Bobby and Raphael were roughhousing on the futon, throwing pillows at each other, calling each other names. They looked like they were having so much fun. Then they settled down and began looking at drawings and sketches, talking and pointing animatedly.

Kenny watched wistfully as they continued jabbering on together. This was a part of Bobby's life that he'd probably never understand or could fully be a part of. There was so much of Bobby that he loved and understood, but this he didn't, and this was a big part of who Bobby was. Stepping away, he went back to work, leaving the two of them alone.

Kenny spent the next hour finishing up his chores, and Bobby finally emerged from the back room, his arm draped around Raphael's shoulders.

"I have to go." Raphael hugged Bobby hard. "It was nice to meet you, Kenny." With a wave, Raphael left the store.

"He seems nice," Kenny said, keeping his voice neutral.

"He is."

Kenny didn't know how to react to Bobby right now. He turned and said nothing, not sure what he was feeling. He needed something to do, so he began straightening the wine bottles in the displays, turning all the labels out.

"Kenny, what is it?"

He stopped what he was doing. "You ignored me."

"I spent some time with Raphael."

Kenny turned around. "You barely introduced me and then disappeared into the back." Kenny kept his cool, but he was definitely hurt.

"I'm sorry." Bobby lowered his voice. "I didn't mean to, I was just so excited to see Raphael." Bobby took a step closer and Kenny saw him smirk. "Is it your turn to be a little jealous?"

Kenny looked at that face and began to chuckle softly. "Maybe." He was, but not of Raphael specifically, just the way

Raphael understood Bobby's passion. He appreciated Bobby's art and supported what he did, but Kenny knew he'd never understand it, not the way someone like Raphael did. It made him feel like an outsider to a part of Bobby's life.

"Well, don't be. It doesn't look any better on you than it does on me." Bobby's hands went to his hips. "Green is definitely not your color." Kenny rolled his eyes as Bobby continued. "I'm sorry."

"I'm sorry too." Kenny went back to his cleaning. "I heard you in the office and it sounded like you were talking a different language."

Bobby leaned really close. "We were. But you and I speak our own language." Kenny saw Bobby look around and then he slid his hand around Kenny's waist, hand cupping him through his pants. "A very special language." Kenny swallowed as Bobby removed his hand.

"I know." Kenny turned to look at Bobby. "I'm not jealous of Raphael, at least not in the way you think. I'll never understand you the way he does."

Bobby crinkled his brow. "Understand me?"

"Yeah, he understands art, which is a really important part of who you are."

"Follow me." Bobby turned and led Kenny to the office where he opened his sketchbook, showing his a drawing of the park. "Look at this. What do you see?"

Kenny shrugged, unsure of how to answer the question. "I don't know. See? That's what I'm talking about."

Bobby was patient and asked again. "What does this say to you?"

"Pretty, sunshine."

Bobby turned the page to a drawing he'd done of Kenny. "What about this?"

"Is that me?" Bobby nodded and Kenny looked at the drawing. "Is that how you see me?" Kenny picked up the drawing and stared at it. "I look kind of sexy."

"You are sexy. That's how you look when you come."

Kenny handed back the drawing. "Will you show that to anyone?"

Bobby chuckled and shook his head. "That's only for me." Bobby handed Kenny another, this was one he'd done of Tommy. "What about this one?"

Kenny looked and immediately responded. "Fear."

"Exactly. See you do understand art. What I draw, what I do, is try to take what I'm feeling and express it visually so I can share it with others. So if you understand me, then you understand my art." Bobby stroked his hand along Kenny's cheek. "Besides, you inspire me."

"I do?"

"Oh yes." Bobby looked through the book and pulled out another drawing, showing it to Kenny. "This is another one that no one else will see."

Kenny swallowed as he looked at the pencil sketch. "I'm naked."

"Yes, you are. This is what I see when I look at you. This is what you make me feel." Kenny stared at the drawing and then handed it back to Bobby. "If you ever doubt how you make me feel or how much I need you, just think of this." Bobby handed Kenny the drawing and closed the sketchbook.

CHAPTER 18

"So HAVE you two had a good week?" Katie leaned against the counter, eyeing the wine on the tasting bar jealously. "Damn, I want a glass of wine. Pregnancy is great, but nine months without wine, working in a wine store, really bites."

Bobby ignored her little diatribe and answered the question. "Yes, I think we both had an interesting week. And you'll be able to savor your vino soon enough." Bobby actually rubbed her tummy, and she smiled as the baby kicked. "Besides, you wouldn't give this up for the world."

Now she smiled. "I have to admit, I wouldn't." She let her eyes wander around the store, watching customers browse. Bobby knew she was itching to ask about the missing wine. He knew she was dying to come out and ask, after all, she'd been dropping hints for the last two days. Both he and Kenny had played obtuse and it was killing her—he could see it every time she looked at the display of Chardonnay on the floor. Bobby had found the bottles she'd hidden in the back of the supply closet, but he'd left them there to torture her for going along with Sean's scheme. Once, Bobby walked in on her and Laura talking earnestly, and he could tell they were discussing whether they should say something. Bobby and Kenny were determined that they weren't going to crack first. "When do Sean and Sam get back?"

"Not until sometime tomorrow. The ship docks today and they were staying in Puerto Rico for one night before flying home."

"Doesn't Kenny have to go back to school tomorrow?"

Speak of the devil. "Yes, I do, but not until late." Bobby felt Kenny goose him. "This one has another week." Bobby jumped away from Kenny's hand, laughing and trying not to act like a lovesick teenager.

"I'll open the store in the morning, and Laura's coming in, so you can spend time with Sean and Sam." That was very nice of her. Then Katie's eyes narrowed as she mock-glared at them. "What's going on with you two? You've both been acting weird for most of the last week."

Both of them put on their most innocent faces. "We have?"

She stared back at them, something dawned on her, and she smiled. "Sean's little—" Katie clamped her hand over her mouth, and Bobby was sure he heard her swear under her breath. They waited for Katie to explain her gaffe.

"Sean's little… what?" Bobby raised his eyebrows quizzically.

"You bastards!" Luckily there were no customers nearby, but she lowered her voice. "How long have you known?"

"Known what?" Bobby was enjoying this, and he could have kissed Kenny for playing along.

"When did you figure it out?" They said nothing, waiting for her to continue. "When did you find the missing wine?" She used her fingers to form quotes. "We practically hit you on the head with it."

Kenny scoffed lightly. "Oh, we figured it out days ago."

"And you didn't say anything?" She actually sounded miffed.

Bobby leaned on the counter. "Next time tell Dad 'no' when he comes up with one of his harebrained schemes."

"Did it work?" Her eyes widened expectantly. Both Bobby and Kenny walked away from the counter without answering.

When they were a few steps away, Kenny leaned close to Bobby whispering, "Should we tell her?"

Bobby looked back at Kenny, his wicked expression reflecting in Kenny's eyes. "I think we should leave that for Dad, don't you?"

Kenny kept his laughter under control. "You're a devil, you know that?" He controlled his chuckling as Bobby nodded.

"Let's get things ready for Dad's return." Laughing together, they headed to the stockroom. Kenny spent the better part of the day returning the stockroom camera to its original position, and Bobby reworked some displays before disappearing into the office, the images in his mind pulling him to his sketchpad.

Sitting on the futon with Chloe curled at his feet, Bobby began letting the images and emotions flow onto the paper. As he worked, he quickly realized that everything he drew was Kenny. His face, his hands, his body, each of them flowed almost magically onto the paper. They really needed to talk before Kenny left, but Bobby didn't know how to bring up the subject or what he should say.

Bobby hated the thought of Kenny going back to school. They'd had a terrific week together, one he wouldn't trade for anything. He loved Kenny. He knew that without a doubt. And Kenny had said loving things and had even told Bobby he loved him. More than anything, he wanted to drag a promise of fidelity and devotion from Kenny. He wanted Kenny to tell him he'd be faithful and that once they graduated they'd figure out what they were going to do and that they'd be together. But he couldn't do that. Kenny deserved to be able to explore all the possibilities after he graduated and not be tied to where Bobby was. He hoped Kenny would want to be with him, but he wouldn't force him. And he needed to give him the freedom to make up his own mind.

"Bobby, we'll be closing in less than an hour." Kenny's voice filtered in from the stockroom.

"Thanks." Bobby choked back the emotion that threatened to come to the surface and quickly gathered up his papers, shoving them into his sketchbook before putting everything in his bag. "I'm going to take Chloe for a walk. I'll be back in a few minutes." He really needed to clear his head. Hearing the word "walk," Chloe started prancing around the office until Bobby had his coat on and fastened the lead on her collar. He left the office and walked through the stockroom, getting a kiss from Kenny before continuing through the store, where he waved to Katie as he exited onto the sidewalk. Chloe seemed in an energetic mood, so Bobby walked her around the block until she took a turn and pulled him down the alley.

She kept her head down, sniffing, as they walked past the back door of the store where they'd found Tommy a few days earlier and past the Dumpster where they'd found Charlie going through the trash. "Dad's plan worked, didn't it, Chloe?" She looked up at him and then went back to her exploring. Not only had Sean's ruse gotten him closer to Kenny, closer than Sean had intended to be sure, but he'd also rescued Tommy, helped Charlie, and in turn, been able to get some closure with his father. None of which would have happened if they hadn't spent those evenings casing the alley for a nonexistent wine thief.

Kenny—his thoughts raced back to Kenny. The boy he'd loved since they were seventeen years old. "Thanks, Dad." Even if this was all he ever had with Kenny, he knew he'd remember it for the rest of his life. Kenny, who'd inspired his work, opened his heart to love for the first time, and who supported him in a way only Dad and Sam had before.

To top it off, he'd gotten inspired and finally knew where he wanted to go with his art. He just hoped Dad would go along with the idea.

As Chloe headed for home, she led him to the front door of the building, and Bobby stood out of the light, watching as Kenny walked through the store, his tall, broad frame highlighted in the lights. The man was incredible and everything Bobby had ever wanted. Both his heart and his mind told him that—screamed it to him, as a matter of fact. Tonight was their last night before Kenny went back to school. "I don't know about you, Kenny Johnson, but I intend to make tonight a night you'll remember until you die." Chloe looked up at him like he was nuts, talking to himself. He almost agreed with her as he pulled open the door.

KENNY felt a pair of eyes boring into him. Turning from the display he was filling, he looked out the front store windows into the night. He could just make out the silhouette of Bobby and Chloe standing just beyond the light that spilled out onto the sidewalk. There was no doubt in his mind that Bobby was watching him. He could feel it deep inside like a sensation warming him from within.

Tonight was their last night together. Tomorrow he went back to school, and in a week, Bobby did as well. Taking a deep breath and releasing it, he wondered what he was going to do. His heart hurt at the thought of leaving Bobby. He kept telling himself it was only for a few months, but he knew it could be much longer, maybe forever.

"Should I take out the trash?"

Jimmy's question pulled him out of his thoughts. "Yeah." Kenny finished filling the display and carried the empty wine case to the back with him, breaking it down before unlocking the door. He half watched Jimmy as he put out the trash, locking the door when he was done.

"Will Mr. Bielecki be back tomorrow?"

Kenny hesitated in his reply because he hadn't been paying attention. "Sometime tomorrow, yes."

"Katie said you found the wine." He looked up at Kenny, looking nervous. "Mr. B told me to do it."

Kenny smiled and clapped Jimmy lightly on the shoulder. "I know. It's cool." That seemed to be what Jimmy needed to hear, because he smiled and began sweeping the stockroom before continuing out front.

Kenny followed him out front and saw the front door open, Bobby and Chloe coming in from outside. Bobby unclipped her lead and Chloe made a beeline for her dish, eating, drinking, and then prowling the store before settling back on her cushion. Kenny saw his own doubt and worry reflected in Bobby's eyes, and he was tempted, very tempted, to tell him everything he was feeling. But he couldn't. If Bobby knew, he wouldn't continue at school—he'd move back to town to be with Kenny. And he couldn't have that. He'd rather lose him than hold him back. Was that love? For Kenny it was. The people who loved him, his dad, Sean, Sam, had always put him before themselves. How could he do anything less for Bobby? "I can't."

"You can't what?" Bobby asked as he passed by, taking off his coat.

"Nothing, just mumbling to myself." Kenny checked his watch just for something to do. "We close in half an hour." Katie had already gone and Jimmy was just about done. "Hey Jimmy, is your mom picking you up?"

"No, I've got the car." He continued sweeping.

"When you're done, you may as well go." The smile he got was huge and Kenny turned to Bobby for an explanation.

Bobby stage whispered, "He's got a date."

That explained the smile he'd been sporting for most of the evening. "Go on, have a good time," Kenny said. Jimmy put the broom away and got his coat on. He rushed out of the store, saying his good-nights as he passed through.

Alone in the store—except for a few final customers—Kenny and Bobby got ready for closing. After ringing up the last customer, they closed everything and headed to the car, Chloe prancing excitedly.

"Our last night together...."

Kenny looked at him. "We're only going back to school," he said. "It's not as though we won't see each other again."

"I know, but I'm staying in school, and you'll go on to the academy. We'll barely see each other."

"Bobby." Kenny started to say what he was feeling, but Bobby hushed him softly.

"I feel the same way you do, but I won't stand in your way any more than you'll stand in mine. I was ready to come home and work, but you convinced me to stay in school." Bobby sounded resigned, rather than excited. "We could say we'll be together somehow, that things will work out, and maybe they will." Bobby's hand stroked over Kenny's cheek as he drove through the darkness. "But maybe it won't. I'd give up art school for you, but I know you won't let me."

"Bobby," he said, using his "I know best" voice. "You can't give up this opportunity. They're offering you a full scholarship and a T.A. position. You could make so many contacts and meet so many other artists." Kenny knew he wasn't telling Bobby anything new. He also knew that Bobby was thinking with his heart, just like he always did. "We'll figure something."

Bobby nodded, unconvinced, but remained quiet in the seat next to him. Pulling up to the house, he parked and Bobby got out, silently leading Chloe up the walk and into the quiet house.

Kenny followed. After hanging up his coat, he went right upstairs to his room. Reluctantly, he opened the closet and pulled out his suitcase, packing his things as quickly as he could. When he stopped hearing movement and noises downstairs, he finished packing and closed the suitcase, putting it back in the closet.

He'd just finished when he heard footsteps on the stairs. Kenny waited and then his door opened slowly, a hand flipping off the light. Then the door opened fully and closed, just before he felt Bobby move into his arms, his lips finding Kenny's in the dark. Hands roamed and stroked as they moved toward the bed. Clothing fell away and Kenny felt Bobby's warmth against his skin, a silky hardness pressing against his hips.

"What do you want, love?" Kenny barely managed to keep his voice from cracking as Bobby's hand stroked along his length.

"You, just you."

Kenny moved them onto the bed, lowering Bobby to the cool sheets before joining him, his lips moving over Bobby's, his tongue sampling the rapturous heat of his mouth.

Small whimpers broke the silence of the room and accompanied the caresses of silken skin. Kenny felt Bobby roll over beneath him and found himself pressing his chest to Bobby's back and his length sliding along his lover's cleft. Kenny's lips kissed a winding trail over Bobby's skin. The tender spot on his neck, wide shoulders, ticklish sides, the small of his back, all passed beneath Kenny's lips and ravenous tongue. Warm hands caressed and parted firm cheeks, tongue licking down the cleft as the symphony of whimpers crescendoed into a chorus of passionate pleading.

Kenny needed to see Bobby, connect with him. Tapping Bobby gently, he shifted onto his back, and Kenny could feel Bobby's body thrumming and vibrating with desire as he sheathed himself and slowly pressed into his lover's body. Scorching heat enveloped him as he sank deep, leaning forward to capture Bobby's lips with his. The chorus of pleasure continued to grow, encouraging Kenny as their rapture began and built. Kenny locked his eyes on Bobby's as their bodies moved as one. He loved this man and he needed him to know that down deep, to be able to feel it in his heart, not just hear it with his ears.

Kenny felt Bobby arch beneath him, crying out as his body clenched under him, pushing Kenny over the precipice and sending them both soaring as he cried out against Bobby's lips.

He couldn't move, didn't want to, either. Moving would break the connection between then and Kenny wasn't ready for that, not yet. Reluctantly, he pulled away and slipped from Bobby's body with a small gasp and a feeling of loss.

Kenny slipped away, and after a quick cleanup for both of them, curled back under the covers next to his lover, gently caressing his warm, smooth skin. Kenny felt lips caressing his skin, ghosting over him so softly that he almost couldn't feel it. Despite Kenny's best efforts, sleep overtook them, carrying them away, letting the few hours they had left together pass in the blink of an eye.

CHAPTER 19

BOBBY woke to a number of things: Kenny holding him tight, still asleep next to him, Chloe pressed against his legs, along with noises and movement in the house. Lifting his head, he checked the clock as a thunk reverberated through the first floor of the house. "Kenny," he said, sounding a little panicked, "Sam and Sean are home."

Those bright eyes popped open as they heard footsteps on the stairs. "Bobby, Kenny. Are you up yet?" Sean's voice carried into the room.

Bobby started to get up but Kenny stopped him. "It's okay. We're not a couple of school kids, and I'm not ashamed of you or what we did."

"But you were worried...."

"Not any more." Kenny pulled him close as the bedroom door opened, and Chloe started prancing on the bed.

"Kenny, are you up? Have you seen...?" Sean's voice trailed off, and his mouth hung open when he saw two pairs of familiar eyes staring back from Kenny's bed.

Kenny started to laugh, a deep belly laugh that caught Bobby as well. "Yes, I have Sean, he's right here."

The surprised look intensified. "Oh." No one moved and their laughter trailed off.

"We'll be down in a few minutes, Dad," Bobby said, trying to keep the laughter out of his voice. The bed bounced as Chloe jumped down and raced after Sean. "Looks like we should go face the music." Kenny started laughing again and Bobby joined in. "Did you see the look on Sean's face?"

Kenny's chuckles died down. "He looked as surprised and shocked as I've ever seen him."

Bobby started giggling again. "Even more shocked than the time he found me rolling naked on a huge canvas in the basement so I could see what my body print looked like."

Kenny nodded and his laughter started again. "Yes, even more than that." Kenny hugged Bobby to him, his laughter dying away as he gave him a slow, sizzling kiss.

It felt nice to have Kenny hold him, and Bobby didn't want it to end, but Dad and Sam were downstairs and they definitely had some explaining to do. Reluctantly, they both got out of bed, and Bobby went back to his room to dress.

They met on the stairs, dressed and ready to face the music. "Let's go." Kenny took his hand and held it as they descended the stairs.

Sean and Sam were waiting for them in the kitchen, talking together, and Bobby distinctly heard, "Looks like it worked better than you thought." They both looked up as Bobby and Kenny walked into the kitchen. Bobby felt like a teenager again, waiting to be punished. Then he looked at Kenny, who looked strong and stood tall. Hell, he looked proud and happy.

Sean looked like he was going to start, but Sam patted his arm, quieting him. "We're not angry, just a little confused and a lot surprised."

"We know," Bobby replied softly. "I think we're a little surprised too." Bobby smiled and moved closer as Kenny squeezed his hand.

Both Sean and Sam looked a little shell-shocked, but Sam recovered first, getting to his feet and hugging both of them. "We'll talk about this later." Sam's hug felt good, and so did Sean's a few seconds later. "We missed both of you."

Bobby sat at the table, Kenny sitting next to him. "We missed you too."

Sean muttered, "Didn't look like it five minutes ago."

"Sean," Sam scolded lightly, "they're both adults and able to make their own decisions." Sam looked at both of them, making Bobby shudder under his gaze. "We do need to talk about this." Both Kenny and Bobby nodded as Sean's expression softened and became less severe.

Bobby turned to Sean, trying to change the subject. "We had a great week at the store, and we found your case of Bollinger, along with the other 'missing' wine."

Sean looked contrite. "I figured a little mystery would get you working together. I was worried you were growing apart." Sean smirked at the two of them. "It looks like my plan worked, just better than I expected."

Bobby got to his feet and wrapped Sean in a hug. "In a lot of ways you'd never expect." Sean looked into Bobby's face waiting for an explanation. "I'll tell you all about it later." Bobby continued, "Katie's opening the store and Laura will be in as well, so we can spend some time together."

Sean yawned. "Thank goodness. We were up at some ungodly hour this morning."

Bobby got up and began making breakfast. "Tell us about the trip."

Sam and Sean launched into a narrative about all the things they'd seen: the ship, the islands, the snorkeling. Bobby finished making breakfast as the stories continued. "Can you believe it," Sam was saying, "Sean went swimming in the ocean and lost his glasses?"

Sean batted him on the arm. "They washed up on the beach."

Sam smiled. "Only after you spent ten minutes panicking because they were your only pair." Sean scoffed and they both began to laugh. Bobby finished breakfast with Kenny's help and placed everything on the kitchen table. It was nice, really nice, having his family all together and happy, even if it was for just a few hours.

"So what happened while we were gone?" Sean inquired as he started eating. Sam looked at him funny and Sean sputtered, "Other than that." Sean rolled his eyes.

Bobby and Kenny spent a while telling Sam and Sean about rescuing Tommy, meeting Charlie in the alley, and even seeing Bobby's father.

"He didn't try to hurt you, did he?" Sean looked like he was ready to call the police, even though they had Officer Sam right next to him.

"No. In fact he seems like a different person. I think we were able to make some sort of peace with each other." Bobby went on to tell them about the trip to the mission and the conversation he'd had with his father.

"Are you going to see him again?"

Bobby shook his head as he responded, "No. We said what needed to be said, and I'm content with that." Bobby got up and hugged Sean. "You're all the dad I'll ever need." He was feeling rather emotional and sniffed slightly as he went back to his chair.

Sam swallowed and took advantage of the lull in the conversation. "So, how about you, Kenny?"

Kenny swallowed his bite before replying. "You mean other than reconfiguring cameras to watch the stockroom and spending a few evenings casing the alley for thieves? Then, no, we had a normal week." They all laughed and continued talking as they finished their breakfast. "The shelving you ordered arrived Friday." Even though the conversation appeared normal, Bobby could feel the tension in the air, and he figured it wouldn't be long before he and Dad had one of their talks.

Bobby was right. He and Kenny had finished the dishes, and Bobby had gone up to his room when he heard a soft knock on his door. "Come in."

The door opened and Sean walked in, closing the door behind him, sitting on the edge of the bed. Bobby knew there was no evading the conversation, so he stopped what he was doing and sat next to him. "You want to tell me what happened?"

Bobby didn't know where to begin, but he tried. "I've been in love with Kenny for years now, but I didn't think he felt the same about me."

"That first Christmas after you went away to college?" Bobby nodded and wondered how he knew. "Something happened that seemed to be the start of the ice age between you two. Do you want to tell me about it?"

"Not really." He'd given it way too much thought already.

"Okay." Sean looked disappointed, but he didn't press.

Bobby felt lost. "Suffice it to say that I love Kenny, but I don't know if it'll work out or not. We're both going back to school, and after that, I don't know." Bobby hugged Sean tightly, "I love him so much, but I don't know what's going to happen."

Sean lifted Bobby's chin. "Maybe this is a good thing. Take some time to think about what you want away from the heady emotional things you're feeling right now." Bobby looked at Sean in a new light. "You're both young and need to experience life. If it was meant to be, then things will work out, and if it isn't, you'll have some wonderful memories and experiences."

"Dad, I love you with everything I have."

Sean smiled. "I love you too, and I know how you're feeling. And I can tell you from experience, if it's real, it won't fade over a few months."

"Even if he has an ex-boyfriend with the sexiest voice on earth?" Bobby smirked.

Sean smirked right back. "Even then."

"I'm going to miss him." Bobby's voice was soft.

"I know, but use what you're feeling and channel it into your work." He could always count on his dad for encouragement. He should have known he'd get understanding and support from Sean. The man had never given him anything else since he'd taken him in. "I'm really lucky."

Sean embraced his son. "We both are, Bobby, in so many ways."

The bed bounced slightly as Sean got up and quietly left the room, leaving Bobby alone with his thoughts and worries.

KENNY was packed and almost ready to go. His bags sat next to the closet door. Now came the hard part: saying good-bye to Bobby. *It's only a few months.* But he knew that might not be true. Their lives were taking them on very different paths, and he loved Bobby very much, enough that he was willing to let him go before he'd let him give up on himself.

To Kenny, Bobby was destined for greatness, and he wasn't going to stand in his way, or hold him back. He'd nurse a broken heart before he'd do that. He heard a soft knock and then his door opened and Bobby stuck his head in. "Are you ready to go?"

"Yeah." Kenny looked around the room, his gaze turning to the drawing of him and his dad above the bed. "Whenever I feel sad,

I look at that drawing and remember all the wonderful times. It helps remind me just how lucky I am."

Bobby moved into the room, shutting the door behind him. "I'm going to miss you so much."

"I'm going to miss you too." Kenny smiled as Bobby moved into his arms. "Where are Sam and Sean?"

"They went to the store to check on a few things." Bobby's lips found Kenny's. He needed him, needed one last time before he left. Kenny lifted Bobby off his feet, and Bobby wrapped his long legs around Kenny's waist. Walking slowly, Kenny carried him to the bed without breaking their kiss.

Bobby's hands pulled and tugged at his shirt, and Kenny backed away slightly, lifting his arms so Bobby could slip Kenny's shirt over his head. Then Kenny began ravishing Bobby's mouth, wanting everything he could get, pouring all his feelings into the kiss.

"Kenny, want you."

He pulled up Bobby's shirt and tugged off his pants, before removing his own. He needed to feel Bobby's naked skin against his own. It was going to be a long time before he got to do this again, if ever. And he was going to make it as memorable, as loving as possible. "Want you too."

"Kenny, don't want to wait." Bobby was begging for him.

Kenny calmed Bobby, his bombshell lover about ready to go off. Stroking his arm, he slicked his fingers and slid them into Bobby's body. A long moan shuddered in his lover's chest as Kenny prepared him. Then he pulled his fingers away and pressed his sheathed cock into Bobby's body. A low groan wracked Bobby's body like an addict getting his fix. "You feel so good, so unbelievable." Kenny couldn't think and let his body take over, moving inside Bobby. Arms wound around his neck as Bobby held on, Kenny driving deep into his lover, wanting to get everything he could, to give everything he had. Bobby's eyes locked onto his as

Bobby pulled him down into a kiss. It was heady. Bobby's kiss went right to his gut, slamming him with all the emotions conveyed in that simple act. Kenny had no doubt that they were making love—he knew it, felt it in his soul.

"Kenny," Bobby whined softly, "please." Kenny ran a hand along Bobby's straining length, stroking as he delved deep into his lover's body. "Yeah." Bobby broke their kiss, throwing his head back, and came with a rush over Kenny's fingers. The sight and feel of Bobby's climax triggered Kenny's, and he came, hard, deep inside his lover.

Kenny didn't want to move, didn't want to break their connection. Eventually, Bobby relaxed around him, and he slipped from his body. "It'll be okay."

Bobby nodded and held Kenny very tight. They didn't have much time and both of them knew it. "They'll be back soon."

"I know. I just don't want this to end."

Kenny rolled over, his face next to Bobby's, their lips touching lightly, tenderly. "It really will be okay." Bobby nodded and Kenny watched his lover's eyes drift closed and then open again. The sound of a car door in front of the house got them moving. They dressed and headed downstairs. Sam and Sean walked in a few minutes later. "How's everything at the store?"

Sean smiled. "Wonderful. Thank you both for all your help." Sean handed each of them a check. "I appreciate everything you did this week."

"You're welcome." Kenny got up and hugged both Sean and Sam before heading upstairs, returning a few minutes later lugging his suitcase down the stairs. "I think it's time." Hugs were exchanged all around and Kenny carried his things to the car.

Turning around, he saw Bobby standing behind him. "Have a good term." He looked miserable.

"I will," Kenny said, pulling Bobby into a hug. "It'll be okay." Bobby nodded like he needed convincing. "I mean it. We'll be fine." Kenny hugged Bobby again, giving him a gentle kiss before climbing in the car. Slowly, he pulled away from the curb and watched in the rearview mirror as Bobby got smaller and smaller, finally disappearing as he rounded the corner.

He hated this. He should have told Bobby that they'd make it work no matter what. Should have held him tight and told him that they'd work it out and be together, come what may. He almost turned the car around, but didn't. This was best.

BOBBY stood at the curb and watched the taillights of Kenny's car disappear. He kept himself from crying, but he wiped his eyes anyway and slowly turned and walked back into the house. He kept telling himself they'd make it work, but then a painful thought crossed his mind. What if Kenny didn't want to make it work? He hadn't said he wanted to make it work—all he'd done was comfort.

Opening the door, he wandered in the house, seeing Sam and Sean sitting in the living room watching television, curled together with Chloe on the sofa. That's what he wanted, and damn it, he wanted it with Kenny.

"Fuck," he mumbled, under his breath. Kenny was doing it again. Pushing him away for what he thought was Bobby's own good. He shook his head slowly as he realized what had just happened.

Bobby headed up to his room, determination replacing the sadness he'd felt a few minutes before. "You did it again." Bobby actually called out to the walls. Bobby picked up his sketchbook and a pencil. As soon as his hand began to move across the paper, with the first line of graphite, he could see Kenny.

CHAPTER 20

"HI, DAD." Bobby walked into the store carrying his suitcase, his step full of energy.

Sean looked up from where he was working. "How was the first week of classes?" Bobby dropped his things behind the counter and hugged Sean tight. "I got things prepped for you like you asked."

"Thanks, Dad." He stepped back a little. "Is Kenny coming this weekend?"

Sean shook his head. "He said he had a lot of work to do already." Bobby felt the hope he'd been feeling fade away.

"I should get to work while there still some light." Bobby picked up his art case and headed to the stockroom, smiling at the stack of supplies Sean had gotten for him.

"BOBBY! How was the train?" Sean finished ringing up his customer before hugging his son hello.

"The usual." Bobby looked around, hope springing up. "Kenny coming for the weekend? I called and told him I'd be home." Sean shook his head and Bobby felt the hope fade away again like it had for each of the last few weeks. "I should get to work while there's still light."

"I called Sam and we'll have a nice dinner after the store closes."

"Thanks, Dad." Bobby went to get his supplies and start work.

BOBBY walked into the store like he had every weekend throughout the semester, but now there was a little less spring in his step. This time he knew Kenny wouldn't be there. No hope sprang up, only resignation and everything it meant. "Hi, Dad."

"Bobby!" He was hugged with the same enthusiasm and love he always got from Sean. "Get to work while it's still light and we'll have dinner later. I want to hear all about next week's gallery."

"Sure, Dad." Bobby smiled as he went to get supplies.

"It looks great, Bobby. You gonna to be able to finish in time?"

Bobby stopped at the stockroom door. "Yup, just need to put on the finishing touches."

"Excellent, we'll celebrate after we close." Bobby disappeared into the stockroom, gathering his supplies with a sigh of resignation. Finishing his senior project should be cause for celebration. He didn't really feel like it, but he couldn't tell his dad. Sean was so proud and excited, so Bobby pushed away the disappointment that had been building the entire term.

CHAPTER 21

"SO, BOBBY," Professor Hansen roamed the gallery where Bobby was installing the work he'd compiled for his senior project. "It looks like you were able to get inspired." He watched as Bobby hung the last piece on the stark, white wall of the school's gallery. Bobby stepped back next to the professor and admired the portrait. "That's some of your best work."

"That's Kenny."

"He must be very special, although it's a little risky to do a nude as your senior project, and a drawing at that." Bobby could hear the admiration in his professor's voice. "I love the movement and the way you played with the light and shadow." He looked at Bobby and then back at the drawing. "It's really stunning."

Bobby began to chuckle. "That's not my senior project. I needed something to hang in the gallery for the exhibition, but that's not what I'm submitting."

Professor Hansen turned toward Bobby, obviously confused. "Then where is your senior project and why isn't it here?"

At that moment, one of the people from the audiovisual department wheeled in a huge monitor and stationed it near the wall, plugging it in and connecting it to the network. "I have everything set up for you. All you need to do is tune it to the video one setting."

"Thank you, you've been a big help."

The technician smiled and left while Bobby turned on the monitor and tuned it. The monitor displayed what appeared to be the side of a building.

"This is my senior project." Bobby went on to explain. "When we met at the end of last term, you told me I needed to dig down into myself, find that part of me that I was keeping locked away, so I did. I call this, 'By the Grace of God…'."

"Where is it?"

"It's on the side of my dad's wine store in Milwaukee. It was a little too big to bring in to the gallery, so we set up a camera for the exhibition. It's really amazing the way it changes with the light."

"How? What?" Professor Hansen began to stutter he was so taken aback. "Everyone looks homeless."

"When I was fifteen, I was living on the streets. My dad took me in and gave me a home. I was one of the lucky ones. I wanted to portray that not everyone is so lucky."

Professor Hansen stepped closer to the monitor, furrowing his brow. "The faces look familiar for some reason."

"They should. I used famous faces, recognizable faces, for all the figures. I wanted to highlight that homelessness could happen to anyone." Bobby pointed to the figure at the lower left. "Except for him. That's Kenny." Bobby looked at the sketch on the other wall. "He inspired it all."

Professor Hansen didn't take his eyes away from the monitor. "He must really be special."

"He is." Bobby felt some of his excitement fade as he did what he'd done a lot through the term… think of Kenny. On the weekends when he'd travel home to work on the mural, he kept hoping that Kenny would be there as well, but he never was—even after Bobby had told him repeatedly that he was spending weekends in Milwaukee working on his senior project. Each weekend, he'd hope, and each weekend he was disappointed. And each weekend, more doubt would creep in that Kenny really didn't want him. That what they'd had that week in March was just that, a wonderful week, but no more. He'd thought about talking it over with Sean, but it seemed awkward, and he didn't want to put either him or Sam in the middle. "He really is special," Bobby said, pulling himself out of his ruminations and returning to the present.

Professor Hansen turned and looked at Bobby quizzically. "Is everything all right?"

Bobby nodded and stepped back, turning away for just a moment. He needed to get hold of himself. The exhibition opened in a few hours and he needed to be up and ready, not mopey and maudlin. Bobby was thankful when the professor wandered off to where one of the other students was putting the finishing touches on her exhibit, and Bobby used the opportunity to escape and head back to his room.

"Hey, Bobby." Raphael's voice was full of excitement. "Just a few more days until we graduate and inflict ourselves on the world. Well, I'll be inflicting myself on the world. You'll be frustrating the instructors for two more years." He radiated so much energy, Bobby expected him to start jumping on the furniture, or prance around the way Chloe did. "Jesus, Bobby, would you stop moping around?" Raphael finally settled on the sofa. "You've been quiet and morose all term."

"I know I should be excited, but…."

"Are you still going on about Kenny? Come on, bud, you had a great week, but he obviously isn't interested." Bobby's misery must have shown on his face because suddenly Raphael was there, hugging him tight. "I'm sorry. I know you're hurting, but you need to get over it. You need to move on." For the first time, Bobby felt tears sting his eyes. All the weeks he'd hoped and had his hopes dashed again and again he'd never cried, but he did now. "It's okay. I know you loved him."

Bobby pulled back and rubbed his eyes, grabbing a tissue from the desk. "I've loved him since I was seventeen." Bobby sniffed as he got a hold of himself. "I guess I should take Dad's advice. He told me if it was meant to be, it would work out, and if it didn't, then I should cherish the memories and move on."

Raphael hugged him again. "I always thought you had the coolest dad ever." Raphael let him go and began getting ready. "We need to be at the gallery in an hour." Bobby began getting ready, feeling a bit better. "Are your dad and Sam coming?"

"They said they were." Bobby sure hoped so. "If not, they'll be here tomorrow. It really depends on Dad's schedule at the store."

Raphael grabbed his things and went into the bathroom, and a few minutes later Bobby heard the shower start. There was a time a few years earlier when he'd have joined him, but they hadn't been together like that since sophomore year. Bobby spent much of the time pacing, and it wasn't until the heard the shower stop that he got himself in gear.

Raphael stepped out of the bathroom, dressed and ready, awhile later, and Bobby took his turn. Slipping off his clothes, he started the water and stepped under the hot spray. Usually he took the opportunity to indulge himself in the shower and his mind immediately conjured up images of Kenny, but his heart just wasn't in it. With a sigh, he soaped up and rinsed before turned off the water. Drying himself, he finished his grooming and pulled on his clothes before stepping back into the room.

Raphael was sitting on the sofa and as soon as he stepped out of the bathroom he threw a pillow at him. "Wanker."

Bobby caught the pillow and pitched it back. "Git."

The pillow sailed at him again, Raphael squealing, "Shirttail lifter."

The pillow hit him on the arm and they both broke down laughing. "We've been watching way too much British television." Bobby smirked as he put the pillow back on the small sofa. "We should get going anyway."

Bobby finished getting ready and pulled on a jacket before leaving the room with Raphael. The walk to the gallery was a short one. There were already students and faculty milling about, talking and looking at the work on display. Bobby immediately began scanning the room. "Are they here?"

"I don't think so," Raphael said. His parents were very wealthy and traveled a lot. Bobby had only met them three or four times in four years. "Did your family make it?"

"They promised they'd be here tomorrow."

"Good." They made their way through the room, talking, shaking hands, gathering and giving compliments. Raphael was almost immediately pulled away by his current boyfriend, Renard, and the two of them joined the crowd as Bobby toured the gallery.

"Bobby." He hadn't seen Raphael approach. "There's something you should see." He led him to where his work was displayed and pointed to the monitor. The bright sun lit the mural and the crowd gathered in front of it. He saw Sean, Sam, Mark, Tyler, Katie, Laura, and even Jimmy, along with numerous other friends. Even his grandparents and Mrs. Gold were there. Everyone had a glass of wine and as Bobby watched they all raised their glasses in a silent, long-distance toast.

"How'd they know I'd see their toast?" Raphael pointed behind him and Bobby turned around just as Kenny closed his phone.

"Hi, Bobby." He stepped to him, looking as happy as Bobby had ever seen him. "I've missed you." Bobby stepped closer and saw Kenny's head tilt slightly. Bobby did the same and then slugged Kenny in the arm. He yelped in surprise more than pain. "What was that for?" Kenny rubbed his arm as he stepped back from Bobby, afraid he was going to hit him again.

Bobby stepped close and Kenny tensed, expecting to get punched again, but he didn't know why. "If you don't love me, that's fine, but you should have the guts to tell me instead of staying away and barely speaking to me for the last ten weeks." Bobby hissed between his teeth. "I deserve to be treated better than that. I treated you better than that." Bobby must have remembered where he was because he stepped back and glared at Kenny.

"Is there a place we can go to talk?" Kenny asked. He kept his voice level, but he could feel his temper rise, and he had to work to push it down.

Bobby continued glaring at him and then peeled away, heading outside. Kenny followed as Bobby led him around the building to Millennium Park. Then Bobby whirled around and crossed his arms over his chest. "Okay, talk!" Kenny didn't know where to start. "Nothing to say? Fine, then I'll start." Bobby took a deep breath. "I've loved you since I was seventeen. You pushed me away when we went to college and it nearly broke my heart, then you shoved me further away that first Christmas."

"I told you—"

"I'm talking now," Bobby said, cutting him off. He didn't give Kenny a chance to interject. "That was fine, at least I knew where I stood, but I never stopped loving you. I dated other guys, but turned them away because they weren't you. I was fine with that, and I would have moved on, but then there was that week in March." Kenny stepped back as Bobby moved closer, trying to keep some distance between them, but Bobby wouldn't let him. "I fell for you, Kenny, and I thought you loved me, but when you went back to school, you cut me off. I've been in Milwaukee every weekend working on the mural and you didn't come to see me once. I've called, but you acted like nothing had changed." Kenny watched as Bobby threw his arms around. "Well, I get it now. You don't love me that way, and you don't want to be part of my life. That's fine. We'll be brothers, seeing each other at the holidays and going on with our lives. I get it now." Before Kenny could say anything, Bobby walked away.

"Don't I get to say something?" Bobby turned around, waiting, fire in his eyes. "I don't know where to start." Kenny saw that

Bobby was getting impatient. "I've been in love with you too, and the week we spent together in March was the happiest week of my life."

"So why push me away? Again."

"I thought I had to. When we went away to college, I knew you'd give up the chance to study here to go where I went because you loved me. I knew that and I kept you at arm's length because of it. You have a gift, and I couldn't bear to be the one who held you back. And I thought I needed to do it again."

"So you pushed me away. You unilaterally decided what was best for me and pushed me away. No, what you did was worse. You let me hope for ten weeks that you loved me and wanted to be with me and every weekend I'd go to Dad's hoping you'd be there and every weekend you weren't. And to top it off, you moved back to ex-boyfriend Clay without even telling me."

"I did not!" Kenny began to feel indignant.

"I called, and he answered your phone in his sexy bedroom voice. "Kenny, Baby, there's someone on the phone for you," Bobby said, imitating the voice he'd heard when he called.

Kenny looked down at the sidewalk, unable to look Bobby in the eye. "I did get back with him, but only briefly, and we didn't do anything other than go out and talk."

"Why don't I believe you?"

"Bobby, have I ever lied to you? In all the years you've known me, have I ever lied?" Bobby shook his head. "I couldn't see Clay anymore because he wasn't you. I tried to see other people, but they weren't you, Bobby," Kenny reached out and Bobby backed up, so he let his arms fall to his side. "I was wrong. I shouldn't have pushed you away years ago, and I certainly shouldn't have pushed you away these last ten weeks. I've been miserable. I missed you every day." Kenny reached into his pocket and pulled out a piece of paper and handed it to Bobby. "I slept with this under my pillow because it made me feel closer to you."

Bobby opened the paper and saw it was the drawing he'd done of Kenny.

"I need you, I love you, and I want to be with you. I submitted an application with the Chicago Police Department so I can be here with you while you finish your MFA. I'll do whatever it takes." Kenny knew he sounded like he was pleading, but he felt like this was his one chance to explain why he did what he did and hope Bobby would understand. "Bobby, you were always what was important. I'm just sorry I didn't make you feel that way. I shouldn't have pushed you away and I shouldn't have made decisions for you—for us—without discussing them with you."

"It's not all your fault. I should have told you what I was feeling and what I wanted instead of keeping quiet. I have a mouth and I know how to use it." This time Bobby moved closer and Kenny didn't stop him.

"So what are you saying? That you'll give me another chance?"

"No, Kenny, I'm saying that I'll give us another chance, but I have to tell you that you don't need to relocate here to Chicago. I've decided not to go for my masters, at least not yet. I want to experience things, experience life, before I do that." Kenny had a protest on his lips that Bobby hushed with a touch. "I've already talked to the school, and they said they'll keep the scholarship open for me."

Kenny moved closer, pulling Bobby into his arms. "You didn't have to do that for me."

"I didn't do it for you. I did it for me." Bobby rolled his eyes. "Not everything is about you." Bobby punched Kenny lightly on the arm.

"Ouch." Kenny rubbed where Bobby had hit him. "I've already got an offer from the Milwaukee Police Department but haven't accepted it yet."

"Are you going to?"

"That depends on what you plan to do." Kenny looked around. "Since you aren't going to be here."

Kenny felt Bobby slip his arms around his waist. "I need to get back to the gallery, but afterward, I want you all to myself." They began walking back toward the building. "You don't have to go back do you?"

"No." Kenny felt like he was walking on air. "I want to be with you too, but what about your roommate?"

"We'll figure it out."

Kenny gripped Bobby's hand, "Yes, yes we will." Bobby grinned back at him, and they re-entered the gallery.

"So did you two lovebirds work things out?" Raphael met them as they walked in the door. Kenny looked to Bobby and his grin told him all both of them needed to know. "Thank god. Maybe you won't spend one week of the term moping." He leaned closer. "I'm staying at Renard's tonight, so you two can have the place all to yourselves." Renard approached and slipped his arm around Raphael's waist. "Don't keep the neighbors up." He laughed as Renard led him away.

"How long do you have to stay?"

Bobby checked his watch, "Another hour should do it."

"Good." Kenny's voice lowered and his mouth got very close to Bobby's ear. "Then you're mine, and believe me, I intend to keep the neighbors up for hours."

CHAPTER 22

THE door banged open as Kenny kissed him into the room. As soon as it closed, Kenny had him laying on his bed, his lips being kissed with an intensity he'd only ever dreamed of. "I missed you, Bobby." A hand cupped his head as Bobby was kissed again. "Every day I thought of you."

Bobby stopped and Kenny pulled away slightly. "Then why?" Bobby felt his eyes fill. Kenny looked away and Bobby turned his head back. "Why Kenny?"

"I didn't think I was good enough for you, that I would be good for you." Kenny met Bobby's eyes, "I'm only a cop. I can't help you, and if you're with me, I'll tie you to a town that's not exactly the heart of the art world." Bobby heard Kenny sniff. "You should be able to travel the world and see all there is to see, meet everyone there is to meet."

Bobby held Kenny by both cheeks. "Wherever you are is my world. Don't you see? We were together a week and you inspired me. Together, we can do anything. But without you, I feel empty." Bobby kissed Kenny hard before continuing. "You say I have a great gift, and maybe I do, but Kenny, you have the key to that gift, because you have the key to my heart."

"But…."

Bobby shook his head slowly. "No buts. Where we are doesn't really matter. The art is inside just waiting to come out, and it will if

I'm with you. Don't you get it? You were trying to protect me and my gift, but what you did took away one of the things that made my gift possible. You're my muse."

Kenny's lips glided over Bobby's as they formed a slight smile. "I'm your what?"

"My muse. Some artists look all their lives for what inspires them. For Monet, it was color and a pond filled with water lilies. For Gauguin, it was the people of the South Pacific. For Mark, it's Tyler, and for me—my inspiration is you." Bobby brought Kenny's lips very close to his. "I'm in need of a little inspiration right now." Bobby locked his lips on Kenny's and he felt a warm hand slide under his shirt, caressing the skin of his stomach. "I love you, Kenny."

"I love you too." Bobby felt Kenny lift his shirt, slipping it over his head. Then he felt hands at his pants, but Bobby took Kenny's hand and stilled it.

"Tonight, you're mine." Bobby slid off the bed and onto the floor before getting to his feet, looking down at a stunned Kenny before leaning forward. "Roll over, Kenny." Bobby watched as Kenny turned onto his back. "Take off your shirt." Kenny's eyes widened at the demanding tone, but he complied. "Now lay back and put your head on the pillow."

Bobby ran his hands over Kenny's skin, stopping to work the soft nipples into hard buds before using his teeth to sensitize the skin and his tongue to sooth it. Kenny whimpered softly and thrust his hips on the bed. "Bobby, you're making me crazy."

"I know. Enjoy it. I know I am." Bobby went back to his erotic torture, licking the cuts of Kenny's abs and kissing trails across his skin. "You taste so good." Bobby kissed Kenny, swirling his tongue in his mouth, transferring the salt and sweat to Kenny, letting him get a taste of himself.

"I taste like you." Kenny pulled him down and deepened the kiss as they pummeled their lips together.

Bobby worked open Kenny's pants, parting the fabric, sliding it down Kenny's hips before breaking the kiss and pulling the pants off. Bobby shucked his own pants and rejoined Kenny on the bed, skin to skin, chest to chest, cock to cock. "Much better." Kenny groaned his agreement as Bobby took his lips again, their kisses building. Bobby felt Kenny's hands slide down his back and over his butt, fingers slipping into his cleft. "Kenny," Bobby scolded lightly as he slid down Kenny's tight body. "I have something else in mind."

Bobby opened his mouth and sucked Kenny inside, working the crown with his tongue. Bobbing his head, he worked Kenny into a frenzy, his lover's hips thrusting lightly. Kenny felt so good sliding over his tongue, and if the sounds he was making were any indication, Kenny was over the moon. He'd missed this, missed the taste of him, the feel of him. Bobby lifted his head, tongue working the weeping slit, Kenny's taste bursting on his tongue. He heard himself moan right along with Kenny.

"I'm so close." Bobby took him deep and hard. He wanted everything Kenny had to give. For the last ten weeks, he'd dreamed of having Kenny in his arms, in his bed, crying out for him. And Kenny did just that as he came, filling Bobby's mouth with the taste of his lover. Bobby took it all, swallowing everything his lover could give him before letting Kenny slide from between his lips. "You're amazing, Bobby."

"So are you, Love, but that was just the warm-up." Sliding down Kenny's body, Bobby lifted his legs, exposing Kenny's opening. Leaning forward, he slid his tongue along the crease, swirling it around the tight pucker of flesh. Kenny's musk filled his nose and overwhelmed his taste buds as he plunged deep. "You're mine, Kenny. Say it." Bobby plunged his tongue deep.

"Yours, only yours." Kenny's head rocked on the pillow as Bobby rimmed him within an inch of his life. Moans, whimpers, groans, and short strangled cries, filled the room as Bobby fucked Kenny with his tongue. "Only you, only you." Kenny repeated as Bobby continued his assault on Kenny's most private place, opening it up to him. Kenny was his, and he had every intention of making that point, every way he could.

"Do you mean that?" Bobby looked into Kenny's eyes, moving so their lips almost touched.

"Yes, I do."

"I got tested and I'm clean. I want you Kenny, want you with nothing between us." Bobby kissed him and then backed away.

"I want that too. I got tested last month."

"Are you sure? Once we do this, you're mine and I'm yours."

"I'm sure, I want to feel you." Kenny's eyes along with his words told Bobby that he wanted this just as much.

Opening the drawer next to the bed, Bobby retrieved a small bottle, and after some preparation, pressed himself into Kenny's body. "This feels so different, so hot." The pressure of Kenny's body gripped Bobby like a burning vice as he started to move. Whenever he pulled out, Kenny's body seemed to pull him back in, like it couldn't bear the separation either.

Bobby leaned to Kenny, kissing him as they moved together, slowly, savoring the feeling of being together again. "Love you."

"Love you too." Bobby could feel the pressure start to build and he did his best to keep it back. He wanted to last longer. This felt so good, so perfect, so right. Kenny began whimpering beneath him.

"I'm close, Bobby, really close."

He picked up the pace, changing the angle, and Kenny cried out. "Say it, Kenny. Say you're mine forever."

"I am," Kenny tensed beneath him. "I'm yours and you're mine."

The room began to sway as Bobby's rapture overtook him. "Say it, Kenny!"

"Forever!" Kenny cried out as he came, shuddering on the bed with each convulsive release. Bobby followed right behind, crying out his own declarations of eternal love as he poured himself deep into his lover. For the first time, they were one—he and Kenny were one.

"You belong to me now." Bobby collapsed on top of Kenny and he felt strong arms hold him tight as they both struggled to regain their breath.

HOURS later, the room dark, Bobby stared up at the ceiling, listening to Kenny's soft breathing. "What's wrong, Bobby?"

"Nothing really, just wondering what this means." *Now that the passion's receded….*

Kenny rolled over, his face next to Bobby's. "It means that I'm yours and you're mine. It means that I was a fool twice for pushing you away, and I have no intention of being a fool for a third time."

"But what about the academy and everything else?"

"We'll talk things over and make decisions together. Things will work out because we'll make them work out." Kenny kissed him softly and then with more heat to punctuate exactly how strongly he felt.

"Don't walk away from me again."

Kenny threaded his fingers with Bobby's. "I won't, I'll walk with you."

ANDREW GREY grew up in western Michigan with a father who loved to tell stories and a mother who loved to read them. Since then he has lived throughout the country and traveled throughout the world. He has a master's degree from the University of Wisconsin-Milwaukee and works in information systems for a large corporation. Andrew's hobbies include collecting antiques, gardening, and leaving his dirty dishes anywhere but in the sink (particularly when writing). He considers himself blessed with an accepting family, fantastic friends, and the world's most supportive and loving partner. Andrew currently lives in beautiful historic Carlisle, Pennsylvania.

Visit Andrew's web site at http://www.andrewgreybooks.com and blog at http://andrewgreybooks.livejournal.com/. E-mail him at andrewgrey@comcast.net.

Also Available from Dreamspinner Press

http://www.dreamspinnerpress.com

Don't miss these other exciting titles

by ANDREW GREY

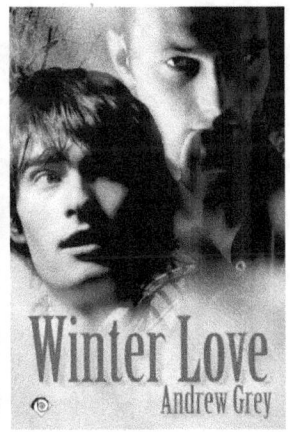

http://www.dreamspinnerpress.com

www.ingramcontent.com/pod-product-compliance
Lightning Source LLC
Chambersburg PA
CBHW070006260626
47159CB00005B/1694